FELL FOR THE OPP

Cj and Dove's Love Story

AUBRY J.

Fell for the Opp

Want to be a part of Grand Pens Publications??

To submit your manuscript to Grand Penz Publications, please send the first three chapters and synopsis to grandpenzpublications@gmail.com

CJ

The loud bass of the music blared through the club speakers; since it was Sunday, and it was new girl training night, it wasn't as packed as it had been the night before when my brother Dozer came through and performed. It was only close family or workers right now. Sitting back in my private booth, I watched as the new girls attempted to work on what they called their routines. Most of the time, the shit was comical, to see a bitch jumped up on the stage and think every nigga in the room was going to stop what they were doing so they could watch them shake their ass. The majority of the time, they would end up with tears streaming down their face as they ran off the stage; either they weren't cute enough, the body wasn't right, or they were weak on the pole. No matter what their time here at Sway's was cut short, and I ended up with a little bit more money in my pocket from betting on which one had what it took or not.

"Yo, I'm telling you, man; I don't see how you do that shit." Benny, my right-hand man, said as he dropped down in the seat next to me. He took a pull of his blunt before slowly exhaling the smoke out and leaning back into his seat. Benny and I have been cool since we were six years old, running through our apartment complex, fucking with the old people knowing once our grandmas found out they were going to beat our asses. But shit, we were young hard-head little niggas just trying to stay entertained since we didn't have too much; we made do with what we had. You couldn't tell us anything about what we were doing, and if you did, you would've been wasting your breath cause we weren't going to listen.

"The shit easy, bro," I said as I took a pull of my blunt. I didn't believe in that sharing shit, especially with another nigga. I broke down my weed, rolled and smoked my shit myself. I couldn't stand to see a nigga roll his shit and just slobber all over the damn thing as he rolled up. Nah, that shit wasn't for me. "Find that bitch with the most confidence, you see her?" I waited for him to check out the entire stage; the newbies stood around in small groups watching as Tatum, the head dancer, showed them some different moves on and off the pole.

"Okay, so shorty in the lime green two-piece, she gotta be the most confident one out there." Benny said as he pointed to shorty, I couldn't even lie. She wasn't too bad on the eyes. Tall, thick thighs, small waist, nice sized titties that looked perky as shit, her skin was a smokey caramel tone with a little red undertone that I bet she always tries to claim she got from her great-grandma on her daddy side cause she Native American. She had what I called dick sucking lips, nice and full with her bottom lip hanging over just slightly, wide expressive eyes but where she fucked up was she wore some fake contacts that made her eye color look the same shade of bright ass green that her outfit was. Her weave was on point, and I only know this cause Benny sister LaTrice been doing hair since we were kids, and she taught me how to spot a bitch whose hair was worth a band compared to bitch who went and got that synthetic shit that smelled like burnt rubber when she tried to straighten it out. Her face and body reminded me of that rapper chick Meg Thee Stallion.

"Good pick." I said, nodding my head; I adjusted my gold-rimmed glasses as I sat up, resting my elbows on my thighs. I watched the shorty for a few minutes. Baby girl was too cocky, wasn't paying attention to Tatum or her instructions. "Baby girl gonna fall flat on her face when Tatum calls her up there. Watch what I tell you."

"Nigga nah, look at her!" Benny shouted as he pointed at her again; he shook his head and waved me off in disagreement. I almost fell over from laughing as his big burly ass jumped up from his seat to watch as Tatum began to pull them to the front one by one to show her if they'd been paying attention. "Baby girl is bad man, watch what my future baby mama does with this beat."

As if on cue, the DJ for the night Life switched to another record, this one by a hot underground rapper named Focus who'd just come onto the scene but was throwing hit after hit out, making folks pay attention. Tatum signaled for Life to drop the lights low and pull up the spotlight, and one by one, the girls showed, or instead, they failed to show her what they hadn't learned.

"You bitches can not be serious right now!" Tatum yelled as she signaled for Life to stop the music and bring up the lights. "Do you know how much money I make a fucking night? On a slow night, a random fucking Tuesday when I want to walk in here for a little extra money to put in my kid's saving, I can pull in close to five bands! And that's when I don't put my name as a headliner when I want to remind myself how I fucking started with nothing but two other mouths to feed and rent due the next fucking night." In her sweats, hoodie, and Tim's, Tatum continued to yell her rant as she made her way off the stage; I could see the annoyance and aggravation on her face as she dropped down in her seat. "Yall wasting my fucking time, I could be at home making my kids dinner and watching some shit on Netflix, but no Smooth got me here trying to help you bitches! Benny!" Turning around, Tatum yelled as she looked around the back for Benny.

"Yeah, what's up, Tay?" Benny yelled from his seat.

"Can you call your uncle and let him know these hoes ain't it and I'm wasting my time?" Tatum yelled back to him. She pushed her hair from her face then shielded her eyes with her hands as she tried to look around to find where we were.

"You sure, Tay?" Benny responded as he pulled his phone from his pocket.

"Yeah these bitches wasting my time, and we know I don't play about my time." Tatum said as she got up from her chair. Without looking down, she grabbed her purse from the table and made her way towards us.

"I can't do the dance you just did, but I can dance." Said the look-alike Meg; she rolled her eyes and popped her gum. "Yo shit was played out. That's why nobody was getting it."

"Bitch, you got some nerves." Tatum said turning around to face her, without missing a beat she dropped her purse back on the table and pointed to Life, who started the music back up. "Yo shit better be the best fucking dance I've ever seen my life. You better be better than Ciara, Teyana Taylor, Beyonce, and Queen Janet Jackson combined."

"I know what I can do." Lookalike said as she crossed her arms over her chest.

"What's your name, baby girl?" Life said into the mic.

4

"Treasure." She smugly replied as she batted her fake ass eyelashes at Life.

"Alright, give her the stage; life calls her to the stage properly." Tatum said as she climbed the stairs to the stage. Nodding his head, Life dropped the lights low once again and pulled up another song, this one by Cardi B that song called "Thru your phone."

Treasure rolled her eyes as the other girls moved from the stage; Tatum stood near the center stage, watching as she adjusted her top before grabbing the pole and slowly dropping down into a split that looked like it hurt her pussy from how hard she hit it on the floor. She struggled to get up, but once she did, she showed how horrible of a dancer she was. She did not catch the beat or complete a full dance move; I mean no full twerk or hip whine. By the time she attempted to climb the pole, I knew she was going to end up hurting herself. I watched in horror and amusement as she got about halfway to the top, she lost her foot and fell backward. The loud bam of her body hitting the floor caused the girls to scream in horror while Benn, Life, Tatum, and I laughed loudly. Without wasting time, Tatum walked over to Treasure; looking down at her, she crossed her arms over her chest and looked down at a shocked looking Treasure.

"Bitch, the only thing you'll be doing near here is sucking dick in the back alley. Get your weak ass off my stage." Tatum said as she stepped over her. "If any of you want to follow behind her then you're more than welcome too. But if you want to learn how to rock this shit out so you can get this money then bring your ass to the stage and pay attention."

Laughing along with Benny we watched as the rest of the girls all stepped over Treasure to follow behind Tatum. A few of the bouncers went to the stage to help Treasure up; weakly, she rose to her feet and was pretty much dragged off the stage. I knew they were taking her to the back so the medic on staff could look her over before they pushed her out the door.

"That bitch was terrible." Benny said as he took his drink from the bartender, shaking her head at him she waited with her hand stuck out because they were all here on a closed night helping with the new girls everyone was covering jobs they usually didn't do. "I don't see how you can call it each time."

"It's the eyes man. I keep telling you that." I said as I handed Dell money for our drinks.

"You worry about the body too much Benny. We keep telling you that." Dell threw over her shoulder as she walked away from us.

"Them bitches that come in here thinking they about to make money off their looks and not they talent ain't ever about shit. Look at Tatum; baby girl came in here hungry when she started three years ago; she doesn't miss any days unless her kids sick or her baby daddy being a punk ass bitch. Baby got talent too, she studies all kinds of fucking dances, stays on YouTube watching them bitches break down dance moves, and then come in this muthafucka and rock that shit out. She knows what she is doing cause she smart enough to figure out what her audience wants to see. She let them get drunk, make they dick hard, and leave them wanting more." I said as I checked my phone, seeing I had a text from my connect about a runner I hadn't seen in a few days, I stood. Without a word, I tossed back the last of my drink and nodded to Deuce my muscle for the night. Benny must've felt my vibe because he got up from his seat and signaled to Life that we were leaving. I grabbed my black fitted KC hat from the table and pulled it on, wiping off any ashes from the blunt I smoked earlier. We made our way out the front door.

"If you let this little bitch come in here and clown yall, I swear I'm fighting each of you hoes myself!" Tatum yelled to the girls; I didn't even turn around to see who she was talking to; it didn't matter cause none of them bitches would be there tomorrow when they opened the doors for the first shift. I shook my head and hit the auto start on my all black 21 Mustang I gifted to myself a little over a month ago.

"Where we headed?" Benny asked as he opened the passenger door; Deuce and a few of my foot soldiers waited for instructions.

"I got word Timber was seen at his little sister's crib a few minutes ago." I said as I dropped down in my seat and closed the door. I watched as everyone, but Benny walked over to the blue Tahoe that Deuce drove and climbed in.

"Nigga got a lot of nerve showing back up after being ghost for a few weeks." Benn said, shaking his head; he opened up the glove box and pulled out the three Glocks I had in there. "Should've stayed hidden; I guess his family like burying them niggas. I heard Johno's people just took out his cousin over 9th street."

"I couldn't care less about Johno's issues, I just want my product." As I hit the start button, I rolled down the window to let the night air in and put my car in drive. Heading to where I knew Timber would be at.

2

Dove

I was late; with the rain and the slow ass drivers, I had about five minutes to park my car in the student parking lot, get across campus, and in-class before my professor started his lecture. Once he opened his mouth, the doors to his room were closed, and no one was allowed entry until the lecture was over. I hated his ass but I knew I needed his class to graduate, and I utterly refuse to.

"Fuck it." I said as I pulled into the staff parking lot; if I got a ticket for parking here, then so be it, but I couldn't be late. After parking, I grabbed my backpack from the passenger seat and jumped out of the car; I sped walk to the lecture hall every so often, checking the time on my phone; three minutes is all the time I had left. Pushing past people who walked slower than the older adults in the mall. I wasn't usually a rude person, but I didn't have time today. I made it to class just as Professor Glass was reaching for the door handle, smiling brightly. I walked past him.

"One day, I'm going to close the door in your smug

little face." Professor Glass said as I passed him to get to my seat.

"Not with the lord on my side you won't." I said with a laugh as I rolled my eyes. Since I'd taken my first class with him during freshmen year, he'd been making the same promise. Taking my seat, I wasted no time pulling out my laptop and books; I smiled up at him as he pulled out his phone, and Air dropped us the necessary notes we would need for the day. It wasn't a hidden fact that he hated my ass, so I took great pleasure in sitting my ass right in the front of his class so he wouldn't have a choice but to see my face each time he looked up from his desk.

"Aye, can we share?" CJ said from beside me; looking over, I tried not to roll my eyes at him.

"Why can't you use your laptop?" I questioned as I pushed mine towards the middle of the table.

"Shit still down". He said with a shrug; his lying ass used the same excuse every time we had to class together; I knew his laptop wasn't down cause he had it with him. Last week he said it was with the IT department and would be fixed the next day, but when we came to class again, he said it was out.

"Nigga you stay lying." I said under my breath as I pulled up the notes.

"I'm serious as shit! I dropped that bottle of water on that bitch this morning." He said as he pulled my chair closer to him. If I were any closer, I would be in his damn lap, pushing away some. I stared over at him, shocked as shit by what he said. "How else was I going to be able to talk to you?"

"You know you could've just spoke like a normal person " I replied as I tapped on the screen to enlarge the picture we were going over.

"You wouldn't give a nigga like me a chance, and you know it." CJ said with a small laugh, looking over at him at again. I held in the groan I so desperately wanted to let out. CJ was fine to the point it pissed me off at times. He stood about 6 foot; he wasn't a big dude though, he was maybe a hundred and ninety pounds, but I could tell he stayed in the gym cause the sleeves of his shirts didn't hang off his biceps. He was the color of a clean penny, square jaw, thick beard, and lips that were so damn juicy and plumped that it looked like he lapped up pussy and when he bit his lip as he did every so often and I got a glimpse of his gold fangs I had to squeeze my thighs together to try and control my throbbing pussy. His brown eyes sat behind a pair of gold-rimmed glasses that I usually think are ugly, but they worked on him. He never was without his durag, so I wasn't sure on the type of cut he had, but I have no doubt he keeps a fresh lineup.

Instead of responding, I rolled my eyes and put my attention back on my work, I knew the type of dude CJ was, and if I weren't careful, I'd be back into a lifestyle I knew I wanted nothing to do with again.

"I KNEW that shit was going to happen." I said as I pulled the ticket off my windshield; without even thinking about it, I rounded my truck, unlocked the doors, and hopped in. I started my car, instantly the sultry sound of Sinead Harnett blasted through the speakers as I pulled off. Since all my classes were over for the day, I headed towards my house, which was located off-campus.

Once I hit the block, I turned my music down a little and took in my surrounding. With exception of last week, it's been straight mayhem. There were a few shoot outs and a fight that had everyone on lookout and edge. Rolling down the window I let the locals see my face even though they knew my truck. I learned a long time ago to not get too comfortable, the hood only loved you so much, you were never invincible no matter how much you thought you were. I waved at Mrs. Jones as she sat on her porch, smoking her afternoon cigarette before she went back in to watch her afternoon stories. I stopped a little past my house and backed into the driveway, another thing I didn't mess around with. If something popped off and I had to get out of here quickly, I didn't want to take time and back out. I needed to be able just to hit the locked, jump in, and rollover any and everything that was in my way; I always backed into any parking spot no matter where I was.

"Ms. Dove, my mama told me to tell you that nigga was banging on your door while you were at school again today." Tiny, my neighbor said from the sidewalk; she and her little gang of friends all stood at the edge of my drive-way, looking a lot older than their age. She popped her gum in the annoying way that girls did, her mouth opening and closing like she was a sheep or cow chewing its cud.

"Thank you for letting me know Tiny, but I highly doubt she said those exact words." I replied as I pulled my backpack out of the truck. Throwing it over my shoulder as I closed the door I watched as Tiny shrugged her shoulders. Her little entourage of friends giggled and smiled at her choice of words.

"She did too Ms. Dove, she said *Tiny, go tell Dove that no good nigga of hers was banging on the door like he was the police again.*" Tiny said, trying to imitate her mothers' voice. "She was talking to my TT about it when he was doing it; she said something about you must have magical pussy or something cause that nigga get in his feelings every few days and pull the same stunt."

"Bye Tiny!" I said over my shoulder as I made my way

towards my door. I refused to acknowledge what she said. If her mama wanted to talk like that around her or to her, then that was her business, but I wouldn't do it. Tiny at the most was twelve, but the way she acted and spoke, you would think she was well older than that. Plus, she was starting to develop a little body; if her mama wasn't careful, one of these old niggas on the block was going to get a hold of her and turn her out.

"Ms. Dove, if you need me to, I can call my cousin and his boys; they can come through and show out! Just say the word!" Tiny yelled out to me as I closed the door.

Rolling my shoulders, I dropped my bag on the couch as I passed it. I untied my bun I through my braids into before my shower and made my way towards the kitchen. I knew it wasn't too much in my fridge to eat since I haven't been grocery shopping, but I had enough to make a quick snack before I dove into my schoolwork. Pulling my phone out of my pocket, I pressed play on my music app and let my favorite rapper Focus bump through my speakers.

⸻

"BITCH I'M TELLING you now, the club is where the nigga is at!" Redd, my best friend said as she pulled different outfits from my closet. She'd shown up just as I was stepping out of the shower. I'd spent the last few hours going over all my notes from class and preparing for finals. I'd only put away my things because I knew that even though Red loved and respected me, she didn't care anything about education, and I would have to hear her mouth about how stupid it was for me to be in school. She thought I was wasting all my good hoe years being in someone's classroom. She stayed in the club and thought grabbing a hood nigga was the ultimate prize.

"Red, the same niggas that was at the club last week will be there this week." I said as I pulled my comforter back on my bed and climbed in. I knew Red well enough to know she was about to go on a long tirade, so I might as well get comfortable.

"Bitch we are not going to our normal club; my cousin, Swiss on my mama's side, called me and told me about this new club on her side of town that's supposed to be popping," Red said as she pushed her long blue weave from her face as she turned to face me. Now I know you are probably thinking, why is her nickname is Red? But she has a blue weave? Well, it's because Red is her name; her mama dated this young blood nigga back in the day and got the word Red tattooed on her like most dumb ass young girls trying to prove her love. Well after that nigga was killed in a drive-by and she moved on with her life. She decided that she would name her first child Red to make it make sense.

"I know how Swiss is, I don't fuck with her like that, and you know it." I said as I pulled a pillow to the side and laid my head down.

"Right, and I already let Swiss know that you ain't scared to bust her shit open if she about them games tonight, but I want to go. So please, Dove, come out with me!" Red begged, jumping into my bed she pulled me close to her and rocked back in forth; she was annoying in the way that made everything funny. Dramatically she rubbed the side of my head as she continued to beg. "Please, Dove! I just need to go out and let loose, my mama and daddy both getting on my nerves, and Jarvis been out here showing his ass with that new ugly bitch he fucking with I need this!"

Reluctantly I nodded my head; she let out a squeal and pushed me away so that she could get out of the bed and continue to look for me an outfit. I laid there watching as she moved back and forth in the closet, pulling out different tops, skirts, jumpers, some loose-fitting, others would be skintight.

The car ride over to the club consisted of Red complaining about her again off-again boyfriend of six years, Jarvis, who even though she kept saying she wasn't out to see if he was there, I knew differently. I didn't understand Red and Jarvis's relationship, he cheated she would get mad, she would cheat, and he would get mad. They'd fight, she'd send her brothers over to see him, then he would send his sisters to see her. Families would be mad, ready to kill each other, and they'd been seen the next day hugged up somewhere like they just hadn't been causing havoc in other people's lives. Their more recent breakup was the longest, and if the rumors were true, he was done and had moved on with some stripper named Treasure. After a while, I tuned out Red's constant chatter and went over everything I'd been studying; I had less than three months before graduation, then off to Vet school.

The club parking lot was packed, niggas were showing out trying to show up each other with their loud music blasting out their speakers as they stood around with their car doors open, talking to each other. Stepping out of the car, I adjusted my black Gucci tailored shorts that stopped mid-thigh; a fitted rose gold halter top, a pair of simple six-inch rose gold barely there strapped heels completed my look. I tied my braids back up in a ball on the top of my head. I wasn't big into makeup, but I allowed Red to apply a small amount to my face giving me a more natural look compared to her preferred over the top look.

"Yo, look at all the niggas up in here!" Red said, grinning. She looped our arms together and pulled me away from the truck. I quickly dropped my keys in my wristlet purse after making sure my truck was locked. By the time we made it to the front door, bitches complained about us cutting in line, and niggas tried to get our names and numbers. I watched with humor as Red whispered something in the door man's ear before he nodded and opened the door for us.

"Girl, what the hell did you tell that man?" I questioned as we moved through the crowd; every so often, I'd hear someone call my name, and I'd wave in that direction, but we never stopped moving. If I stopped for one, then I'd have to stop for everyone, and I'd never make it to my destination.

"That Tika told me I was good to go with my guest and gave him the code word he had texted me while we were headed over." Red tried to say under her breath because she knew how I felt about Tika and her association with him since he and I had broken up. But I couldn't control who she hung out with, especially since Tika grew up with them; he was unofficially family to her and her siblings. He even took a charge for her brother a few years ago and did his bid without question. So I knew that her family would ride for him harder than they rode for me.

"Look, I just used his name because that's what Swiss told me to do. I know you ain't trying to deal with him like that, but I wasn't trying to stand in that long ass line out there and deal with that shit." Red said as she turned to face me; she sucked her teeth at my lack of response and grabbed my hand to pull me along. "You may as well know now that he said he might slide through some time tonight, but I told him not to show his ass, so don't worry."

"Bitch!" I shouted over the music as I snatched my arm away. "You know you wrong for not telling me before now!"

"Look, you need to get out of the house." Red said,

swinging around to face me again; she crossed her arms over her chest and rolled her eyes. "All you do is study, go to class, sit your ass at home, eat, sleep, and repeat. You ain't got no life since you called off your engagement, and you know it!"

"And that's my business! I told you I wanted to study and finish out my degree. How I choose to handle my life now is my business. As my best friend, you should respect that!" I said to her as I walked past her; there was no reason to fight or argue with Red about how I chose to deal with my breakup with Tika. She didn't see the point of not signing my marriage license after Tika and I said our I Do's; she swore up and down that she didn't know he had been cheating our entire engagement, but a small part of me didn't believe her. She wasn't surprised when I called her crying in the middle of the night; I hadn't been on social media that much, and I needed a mental break after a year of dealing with wedding stuff, school, and trying to buy a house. So, I got online just to see what everyone was up to and stunt on a few bitches with some pictures of the engagement ring and even a couple of Tika and me. Since we were set to sign our marriage license the next morning before we left for our honeymoon, I even wanted to update my relationship status. Imagine my surprise when I saw I had a few DM's from bitches I didn't know; I had about three different bitches telling me how they spent time with Tika, some sent pictures as proof, but the one that got me was the picture of Tika smiling down at a newborn baby girl.

"Bitch all I'm saying is you're sometimes boring. We too fine to be worried about some niggas. You had a good one, and you let him go over some shit that happened before yall was married, technically yall was still single." Red said as we made our way into VIP, the music wasn't as loud as the main level, but the weed smell was strong. I knew without a doubt I'd have to co-wash my braids tonight once I got home to get the smell out of them.

Instead of responding to Red, I headed towards the bar to order some drinks; if I were going to be here and possibly run into Tika, I would need a few drinks. Leaning against the bar, I sipped my cranberry and rum mixture; every so often, someone would come up and speak, but for the most part, I stood there looking pretty with nowhere to go or people to talk to.

3

Cj

"Nigga I'm telling you now this fucking place stay packed, and it ain't even been open that long!" Benny yelled over the music as we made our way through the room. The bass from the speaker shook the room every time we took a step, like the shit was in tune with us and not the music. I couldn't front if I wanted to, to be able to walk through my club like I was and know that shit was successful made a nigga feel extra happy tonight. "I had to tell Cole to make sure we not over occupancy count; I don't want the Fire Marshall back in here, giving us a hard time again."

"Smart move." I responded with a nod of my head. I adjusted my gold frame glasses as I looked around; the lower level was mainly used as a dance floor, bitches stayed down here twerking on a nigga, trying to show each other up. The second level was more relaxed and chilled; you could drink or eat at a table. Since it was enclosed with soundproof glass, it gave you more of a restaurant feel, including a hostess and servers. We gave graduates from the local culinary school a chance to work on their skills and prepare and cook meals. "Let's go check on the VIP; I want to make sure that the new bartender we hired is okay and doesn't need anything."

We took the back stairs, checking on staff as we made our way to the upper deck that looked over the dance floor. Benny spoke with security as I checked on the wait staff and hostess, once we made it to the VIP and looked around, I knew the man above had blessed me beyond imagining tonight.

"Cools said VIP is booked out for the night, some nigga named Tika is here celebrating his reunion with his wife or some shit like that." Benny said with a shrug as he looked around, I nodded my head instead of responding as I watched Dove. Dove had to be the finest chick I'd ever seen, and in my life, I'd seen enough to know what I was talking about. Dove was the type of chick I'd bring home to meet my granny, smart, funny, heart of gold, quick with her comebacks, so she always kept a nigga on his toes and fine as hell. She was short, maybe pushing five-two, skin dark like melted chocolate, thick thighs, her waist was small, but she had a small pudge that I loved on a woman. She had maybe DD breast, and her face made my dick jump every time I saw it. Round chubby cheeks, full thick lips, small nose, her eyes were the color of her skin, and she kept her hair in braids so I couldn't tell the grade, but it didn't matter cause her shit was always right. But I think I love the sound of her voice more than anything; that shit was husky like Toni Braxton's. I intentionally sat next to her in class every day just so I could fuck with her, she always acted like it bothered her, but I knew it didn't cause the one day I left her be she kept staring over at me, checking on me to make sure I was okay.

"Hey, I'm about to go check on someone I know." I said to Benny before walking over to Dove. She must have felt me watching her cause she looked up at me; the look of surprise and amusement that crossed her face made me smile.

"Hey." She said softly; she tried to hide the smile that blossomed across her face by taking a sip of her drink. I did a slow assessment of her, starting with her feet; I bit my lip when I saw her small feet in some rose-colored spikey heels; her toes painted a dark purple was a bonus. I let my eyes roam over her legs, noticing a collection of birds and flowers tattooed on her left leg. She wore some black Gucci shorts and a shiny top the same color as her shoes.

"What's up?" I responded as I stopped in front of her. Even though I wasn't the tallest nigga in the room standing next to Dove, I felt like a giant as she looked up at me.

"Nothing, what you doing here?" She questioned as she looked me up and down. "You look good in that outfit." Another thing about Dove, she didn't hide her attraction to me. She wasn't pushy or in my face with the shit, but she always dished out a compliment when she saw something she liked.

"Just trying to match your fly is all." I replied as I ran my finger down her arm; when we were in class, I never touched her, but I always wanted to, so I took the chance. Her skin always looked so soft and she always smelled like lemon pound cake-like she stayed in the kitchen baking that shit up so much that it was embedded into her skin. I intentionally ignored her question; a select few people knew Benny, and I owned this spot, and I want to keep it that way. When too many niggas knew your business, it was no longer yours, and the people who knew often thought they deserved a piece of your shit.

"Here you go." She said, smiling and shaking her head.

"Nigga you talking to the wrong one." I heard from beside me, turning my head only I looked at some high yellow nigga standing there. His chest was puffed out, his fist balled up, and his eyes bounced between Dove and me. I heard Dove let out a small sigh and suck her teeth before she set her glass down on the counter. I didn't even have to look at her to know she'd crossed her arms over her chest and rolled her eyes a few times.

"Excuse me?" I questioned; turning, I stepped in front of Dove, making sure she stayed at my back while facing the nigga.

"That's my bitch." Yellow nigga said loudly; I hated niggas like him. They always wanted to make a fucking seen like a bitch, needing the people around them to think they were bigger than they were.

"Tika, we are not together, and you know that." Dove said as she attempted to move around me. I let her get partially around me before I put my hand on her stomach to stop her from moving past me.

"We squashed that shit Dove, that's why I threw you this party to celebrate us being back together. I let you have your little fun over the last few months, but that shit is dead. You moving back home and we gonna go down to the courthouse and sign the marriage license." Tika said, waving her off. By this time, he finished talking the rest of the guest in the room had noticed our little interaction and was paying attention.

"No, Tika, we haven't," Dove said, shaking her head. "We are not back together; I don't know how many times I have to tell you that, but we ain't rocking like that ever again. If this party is for that then this ain't no party." Dove said, I could see her anger building up as she spoke to him. Out the corner of my eye, I saw Benny and the rest of my boys spreading around the room. I wasn't the arguing type, and if this nigga Tika didn't calm his ass down, I'd air this entire bitch out without a second thought.

"Nah, baby, you got it wrong; we not over until I say we are. You owe me a son, and I plan on getting him." Tika said as he tried to reach for Dove, who must have known he would attempt to grab her because she stepped back just in time.

I pushed her back into one hand, sandwiching her between me and the bar, and with the other, I pulled my Glock nine out of my waist and pointed it at Tika's head. "My nigga we don't touch shit that doesn't want to be touched around here." I said as I pushed his head back a little with the barrel of my gun. The collective sound of guns being loaded didn't deter me from making my point.

"You must not know who you fucking with." Tika said with a smile; my gun at his temple didn't seem to faze him. Like the clown he was, he let out a loud laugh before raising his arms in the air; I took my eyes off him for a second to look around the room. His boys stood there with their guns aimed at me as if I was supposed to be scared. This time it was my turn to laugh.

"Nah nigga you don't know who the fuck you're dealing with." I said to him, nodding my head to my boys that had positioned themselves around the room, their loaded guns to the back of each of his boy's heads. Once he realized what was happening the smirk, he wore dropped from his face. "I'm not the nigga you want to play with. I'll put a bullet in each of yall heads tonight and not lose an ounce of sleep over it. But that's not my decision; that's on Dove. All she has to do is say the word, and I'll destroy the entire world for her." I glanced over my shoulder to her; I watched as her wheels spun, debating if she wanted him gone from her life forever.

"No, let him go." Dove said softly while looking up at me. Turning my attention back to Tika, I shook my head at him; he didn't realize what I said was true. Nodding my head, I dropped my gun to my side with my finger still on the trigger just in case his nigga didn't take his blessing and wanted to meet the man above tonight.

"Take your ass out of here before I change my mind." I said to him as I grabbed Dove's hand and walked out of the room. I give Benny a single nod as we passed him; he let out a whistle as soon as my foot crossed the door frame. I pulled Dove close to me as I moved through the building, we didn't rush but we moved through the crowd quickly.

"Give me your keys." I said as we walked out the front door; she didn't even question me as she pulled them out of her pocket and handed them to me. The door swung open, and Benny stepped through, a big grin on his face as he walked towards us. "Benny is going to follow us in your truck." I handed Benny the keys to her car and pulled her along to my mustang. I opened the passenger door, letting her in and closing it before rounding the car with Benny next to me. I got inside and watched as Benny hit the key fob to locate her car. When the lights clicked on an all-white F150, I watched with humor as Benny glanced back at us then walked to the car. Once he got inside and started it up, we pulled out of the parking lot. At the stoplight, Benny pulled up on the side of us and rolled the window down.

"I know the routine; I won't hit any corners in baby girls shit but just know I want to!" Benny said as he turned up the volume on her stereo system. Since we were so close, her phone linked to the blue tooth, and Focus came blasting through the speakers. He nodded the words as Dove laughed at his antics.

"Alright, man! Be safe!" I said to Benny before pulling off. With my eyes on the road, I pressed play on the touch screen dashboard, and the same song that was playing through her car came on. I looked over at her with a smirk on her face. I dropped the top as we hit the highway, the night was young, and I had the finest woman in the world sitting in my passenger seat. The night was going to be good.

"I'm hungry." Dove said, she relaxed into her seat and closed her eyes.

"I got you, don't worry about it. I know the best place in the world to eat, and it's always open." I said as I switched lanes.

"I trust you." Dove said softly.

<u>Dove</u>

WE PULLED into the driveway of a cute little ranch style house that was located about thirty minutes outside the city. I knew the area because my favorite auntie lived out this way, and as a kid, I would spend every summer with her. I watched CJ as he got out of the car, rounded it, and opened my door, and just like the gentlemen I figure he was, he held his hand out to help me get out of the car. With a smirk on his face, he closed the door and gently pulled me behind him. He unlocked the front door and stepped inside. The smell of fried chicken and greens hit my nose immediately, making my stomach growl. I hadn't had a home-cooked meal since the summer when I visited my aunt; her husband stayed in the kitchen cooking.

"Put your shoes over there and slid a pair of house shoes on. Granny doesn't like outside dirt on her hardwood floors." CJ said, pointing to a chair that I could sit in, I did what he instructed and slid my feet into a pair of black Nike slides that were way too big for my feet, but I preferred slides to house shoes.

"I said house shoe man, they all clean and new." CJ said, chuckling as he looked down at my feet. I knew he expected me to put on the house shoes, and I would have, but I had a feeling the slides were his, and I wanted to ruffle his feathers just a little bit.

"These are what I consider house shoes." I said smiling at him as I raised one of my feet side to side to show him the shoe. He wiped his hands down the lower half of his face and licked his lips. I could tell I wanted to say something to me, but instead, he smiled and nodded his head.

"Alright, cool, come on then." CJ said after kissing my forehead; he put his hand on the small of my back and lead me through the hallway towards the kitchen. As we walked, I took a moment to take in the house; it was lived in; it felt homey and loved. We stepped into the kitchen. An older woman sat at the table, coffee in one hand, and her head deep into a book. Her head popped up when she heard us approach, and a smile identical to CJ's blossomed onto her face.

"Well, isn't this a nice surprise?" She said as she stood from her chair.

"Hey, my baby." CJ said as he pulled her into a hug; she squeezed him hard and rocked side to side. She let him go and cupped his face in between her hands; she smiled up at him before pulling him into another hug. I could hear her softly thanking the Lord for allowing her to see her baby again before letting him go and smiling over at me.

"Well, aren't you the prettiest little thing I've ever seen?" She said before coming to pull me into a hug. It was something about a mother or grandmother hug that did something to your soul and this woman had the touch. "I'm CJ's grandmother Clever. It's nice to meet you, honey."

"It's nice to meet you too Ms. Clever, my name is Dove." I responded as I let her go. Ms. Clever smiled at me as she patted my cheek. I looked over at CJ then at his grandmother, who didn't look nearly old enough to have a grandchild in his mid-twenties.

"You hungry baby? I know if CJ has come over without me calling him first, then that means he is hungry and expects me to cook for him." Ms. Clever said as she made her way to the fridge; without waiting for me to answer, she began to make us both a plate. The chicken and greens that I smelled when I first walked in looked so good, I would've eaten them cold. "Go on and wash your hands and then sit down. The food should be warmed up by then." Ms. Clever threw over her shoulder as she waved us off. "CJ show the girl where the washroom is and don't be in there playing like you did as a kid."

"Yes ma'am." CJ said, smiling as he pulled me gently behind him. As we walked the short distance to the half bathroom off the kitchen, I took a better look around me. I was right when I said the house was homey and loved; there were pictures of CJ as he grew up along the wall and a few others of more kids and even a couple of Ms. Clever.

"She likes your vibe; if she didn't, she wouldn't have offered you any of her food." CJ said as he dried his hands on a decorative towel that hung near the door. I let my mouth drop in surprise as he shrugged his shoulders and guided me out the door and back to the kitchen.

"Food is almost done, take a seat. You want juice or

water, CJ?" Ms. Clever questioned as we made our way back into the kitchen. Again, she didn't wait for a reply as she pulled two bottles of juice and water from the fridge and set them on the table. CJ pulled my chair out for me and I sat down.

We sat down and ate, enjoying our conversation and getting to know each other. I learned that Ms. Clever raised CJ since he was seven, his father, who was Ms. Clevers son never settled down long enough to raise a child and his mother was a crack head who was still in the streets. The dynamic of their relationship warmed my heart; it is evident that CJ loved his grandmother and vice versa.

"Oh good Ms. Clever, I am stuffed, but everything was so good." I said as we headed to the door; I had a to-go bag with leftovers as well as a piece of chocolate cake that CJ pouted over when his grandmother offered it to me.

"Thank you for the compliment, baby girl." Ms. Clever said smiling as she opened the door. She pulled me into another tight hug and whispered in my ear to come back whenever I wanted. Her door was always open before letting me go and doing CJ the same way.

"Dove, honey, I've meant to ask you what your last name is. You look familiar and was just wondering if I knew your people." Ms. Clever questioned.

"My mama is Rose Lincoln." I said with pride; I'd intentionally left out my last name when I introduced myself earlier. Even though my last name was a common one, it wouldn't be hard to put the pieces together and realize I was one of the six Lincoln kids, and everyone knew our history. Instead of waiting on the stares and insulting words, I knew that was bound to come up; I quickly gave Ms. Clever another hug and walked to the car. I didn't run or rush to the car; instead, I walked with my back straight, shoulders square, and head held high. Without asking, CJ unlocked the car from the porch, and I got in. I watched as he said a few parting words to his grandmother, gave her another hug, and headed to the car. Inside he didn't say anything as we drove away and I didn't blame him. If someone would've told me that the person, I'd just spent time with daddy was snitch and mama was doing a bid, I wouldn't have shit to say to them either.

4

Cj

I drove in silence for the entire drive back to my house, thinking about what Dove told my grandmother; her parents were notorious. Growing up, everyone knew about the Lincolns, they ran the hood, and no one wanted to go up against them. They were hood royalty but wasn't cocky with the shit; they gave back threw block parties for the kids before school started, handed out turkeys and hams for the holidays, and even gave out Christmas presents. I grew up thinking they were more powerful than the President with the pull that they had. Then one day, all that shit was over; Mister Lincoln, Dove's father, flipped and became an informant for the DEA. Nigga even snitched on his wife and mother of his kids, Rose. During the trial, while he sang like a damn bird Rose sat there, head high, face blank, and never opened her mouth whenever they asked her a question. They ended up putting Mister in protective custody and moving him out of state, but Rose is doing a twenty-year bid. The hood called her the real OG of the family and gave her nothing but respect; I even know a few OG's that put money on her books on a regular because she did what a rider was supposed to do and kept the secrets. Mister, on the other hand, thought that the hood forgot but we haven't. Eventually, he will pop back up. And when he does, I know at least twenty niggas that plan to put a bullet in his ass for dragging people down with him.

"Why you ain't run like yo daddy did?" I questioned while we were stopped at a light; looking over, I watched as Dove turned her attention from the window to me. The anger that flashed briefly in her eyes lit a fire in me I didn't even know was there.

"That nigga ain't my daddy." She replied. The coldness in her voice let me know that there was something she didn't say. Nodding, I turned my attention back to the road as I pulled forward.

"Yo, mama was married to him, that nigga was her husband, so that makes him yo daddy." I said to her, sucking my teeth. I tried to control my temper.

"That nigga nutted in my mama, and a few times the seeds took, resulting in Lily, Sage, Falcon, and myself, but that doesn't mean he, my daddy." She said still with an attitude. "That nigga lost the privilege to call us his offspring; my mama was there the entire time he wasn't."

"He snitched on yo mama." I said. I turned down the music as I got closer to my neighborhood, even though it wasn't loud I still respected the peacefulness of the neighborhood as I drove through.

"He did a bitch as thing cause my mama was leaving him; she was tired of his shit and knew he was stopping some of her money. He only found out about it cause a chick she swore was her friend was running her mouth to him." Shaking her head, Dove let out a frustrated breath. "Everybody in the hood knew my mama was the brains behind the shit he was doing, but she was happy, so none of my uncles thought it was a problem."

"But it was." I said as we backed into the driveway; I hit the garage door opener and allowed it to open before I backed into my spot and closing the door. We sat in the dark for a while; I pulled out my phone and hit Benny up, letting him know we were at my spot. He replied, letting me know where he left Dove's keys in my kitchen and that he had a few more stops to make before heading to his crib.

"Lincoln did what everyone expected a bitch to do, got jealous, and hurt her the best way he knew he could. He snitched on her and the dude she was fucking with, or at least who he thought she was fucking with. My mama doing a twenty-year big while that nigga on a beach somewhere enjoying his life." Dove said as she turned to face me; even though it was dark in my garage, I could still see her from the moonlight that shone through the panels on the garage door. "My mama taught us how to love, support, respect, and stand by your man, but she also taught us to never be a fool for one. She grew up in the streets, knew the game better than most niggas, and they respected her because of it. Her daddy was street nigga, his daddy before that too, so the Ballard's made a name for themselves before he brought his weak ass around."

Nodding, I unlocked my door and got out; I respected a person who knew what they were about. She was right. Her mama people were legends before her daddy came around; she was the true one of the family, and her actions showed that. I opened the door for Dove, and we went inside; my house was my sanctuary, and I didn't let too many people know where I laid my head, but I had a good feeling about Dove. I dropped my keys on the kitchen table, tapping on the tank of my iguana as I passed it. I could hear Dove behind me, her heels clicking against the hardwood then being practically silenced as she stepped onto the carpet.

"Look, I could see myself fucking with you hard." I said as I pulled my tray from under the coffee table; Dove sat next to me as I broke down my weed. "Aint no one questioning yo loyalty, especially if you broke it down like that about your mama family. I grew up admiring them niggas; when your uncles would pull up, it was like a party each time for the kids, so I know you about that life and see what I'm about. I just need to see if you okay with fucking with me. Yeah, a nigga like me getting his education on that's why I'm in a couple of your classes, but I'm still a street nigga at the end of the day, even with me trying to do better. After what your pops did to your moms, I can understand why you trying to stay out the streets, and I will respect it."

"So, you a fan of my family, huh?" Dove jokingly asked, she knocked her shoulder with mine as she lit her own blunt that she pulled from her purse while I was rolling my blunt.

"Man, that's all you heard me say?" I questioned after I took a pull of my blunt. Shaking my head, I watched as she fell over laughing; the joy and happiness that radiated off her in that simple moment did something to me. Even if we didn't end up together, I'd rock with Dove every day just to make sure she laughed like that.

"Hell yeah!" Dove said as she did a little twerk in the seat after she sat back up. I shook my head at her as I pulled at my blunt again. "You want to rock with a real bitch? I get it." She said this time nodding her head and wiping the tears that developed from her laughing so hard. Taking another pull of her blunt, Dove eyed me before blowing her smoke towards me. "*If I was you, I would want to rock with me too, nothing like having a chick who knows the street life and is book smart. Gotta have a bitch that can suck your dick every day and your granny still love her."*

"Man, shut up, and come here." I laughed as I pulled her closer; she willing came to lay her head on my chest as she hummed the lyrics of the new Focus and Tinner song that we'd listened to on the way over here. Eventually, I reached over and turned the lights off, the only sound from an unexpected downpour and our blunts kept us in a chill state.

"You got a go-bag in your car?" I questioned after a while, it was late, and I didn't plan on her driving back to her spot, so even if she said no, she was still staying. I wanted to sleep next to her, wake up, and start our day over still in each other's chill vibe. I wasn't lying when I told her I could see myself fucking with her heavy, and I planned to show it.

"Yeah, never leave home without one." She said, nodding against my chest.

"Cool, my room is upstairs to the right. You can go ahead and head up; I'll grab your bag and bring it to you. You need anything else out of your truck?" I questioned as I stood up; I pulled my black shorts up, adjusting them on my waist before helping Dove from the couch. She gave me a small nod before heading up the stairs, I watched her as she made her way inside. I grabbed her keys off the island where Benny told me he left them and grabbed her white bike duffle bag and her blue Nike bag. I knew it was her school bag because she always had it with her.

Once I made my way back into the house, I checked the locks and security cameras before making my way into my room. The lights were still off, but I could hear the shower going, so I headed that way to bring her overnight baby.

"Hey, I got your bag." I said as I knocked, I pushed the door open a little just in case she didn't hear me and I needed to say it again.

"Can you put it on the toilet?" She said over the water. "I'm using your soap since it has my name on it."

"Yeah, I grabbed your school bag too. I know you don't have class until Monday, but I didn't know if you planned on studying while you're here." I said as I dropped her bag down, turning towards the shower, I said a silent thank you to the fact that I had a clear shower door instead of a shower curtain. I let out a small laugh at her mention of the soap. I used Dove sensitive soap, so I knew exactly what she was talking about.

"Thank you! I planned to study in the morning, so that helps a lot." Dove said as she continued to wash her body. Before, I never saw the joy in watching a woman bathe; it was like wash your ass and get out. But with Dove it was something about watching her that made my dick hard, she wasn't a BBW. More of a slim thick, and I loved that shit. I didn't even move when she cut the water off and open the shower door; instead, I reached over and grabbed her the extra-large bath sheet that was on the countertop. She raised her brow in question when I opened it but didn't hesitate to step into it so that I could dry her off. I dropped to my knee, lifting her foot. I let it rest on me as I dried her leg, starting with her foot. I worked my way up her making sure to dry everything as I made my way up. When I got to her waxed pussy, I gently patted it dry, then placed a kiss right on top. I could hear her breath quickly as I licked at her warm crease. I pulled back and put her leg down; I did her left leg the same way as her right, drying it completely off and kissing her pussy once I was done.

Standing, I never took my eyes off hers as I dried her

stomach, then titties; I pinched her hard nipples when I was finished, which caused her eyes to roll in the back of her head. I dried her arms, then shoulders before turning her around to dry her back and ass. Turning her back around, I grabbed the lotion off the counter; I put some in my hand and rubbed them together to heat it before putting it on her body in the same order. I dried her off her front before turning her around again. This time I turned with her so that she was facing the mirror and I stood behind her. I wanted her to see me, a man who worships her body most simply. With her back to me, I put lotion on her back and shoulders before dropping down to my knee again. I palmed her ass in my hands, then kissed each one. I reached up to push her forward, and she went willingly caused her butt to poke out, and I could see her wet pussy. I licked my lips as I watched her juices roll from her pussy down her leg. Without a word I kissed her lips, pushing her creases apart with my tongue. I went to work, licking and sucking on her pussy like it was my last meal.

"Sss. Damn it, CJ, that shit feels so good." Dove said as she slapped at the countertop and rocked her pussy in my face, and like the nasty nigga that I was, I loved that shit. I let her juices flow to my beard as I pushed my tongue further into her. I worked my shit like I was a Que dawg on the yard giving a damn show. I felt her as her pussy started to clench up, signaling that her nut was near. Once her orgasm subsided, I pulled away, I smacked her ass as I dropped my shorts and boxers.

"You better tell me now if you don't want this shit to go any further." I said as I stroked my dick, I was hard as hell and I but I needed to make sure she was on board with this before I slid in. Instead of answering she lifted her leg on the counter and poked her ass out more. Dove looked at me through the mirror, bit her lip, and nodded her head. "Nah, baby, I need you to tell me what you want."

"I want yo-" I didn't let her finish her sentence before I slid the tip of my dick in; her shit was so warm and tight that I had to stop myself from slamming into her. Pulling back a little, I teased her with a few short strokes before sliding in, and yall I swear on everything I know and love, I saw stars. Dove's shit was better than anything I'd ever felt before, and she responded to my shit like it was the best for her too. Finally, after I knew for sure she was adjusted to my shit, I went to work and had her yelling at the top of her lungs by the tenth stroke. I reached up and wrapped my hand around her throat, pulling her towards me. I watched her through the mirror as I stroked her shit. But baby wasn't about to be outdone; once she caught the rhythm, Dove was throwing her shit back with a vengeance, and I was moaning like a fucking fool, and I have no shame in it.

"Give me another nut." I whispered in her ear. I could feel her tightening up on my dick, her leg that was supporting her weight started to shake, and I knew another one was coming. Adjusting myself a little lower, I angled my hips and slowed my stroked until I found the squishy spot I was looking for.

"Oh, oh, oh." Dove moaned as I went to work, she tried to reach back and push me away, but I let go of her throat and grabbed both her wrist and held them behind her back. "CJ, please." She begged me as she looked at me through the mirror. With every stroke, her eyes rolled further and further in the back of her head.

"Give it to me Dove." I said as I moved faster. I could feel my nut begging to be released but I wasn't about to cum until I knew she got hers again. "Dove give me my nut." As if on cue, she released her nut; I looked down and smiled as I watched her squirt all over the countertop. I followed behind her, letting my nut go right inside her.

Dove

I SAT on the couch flipping through the different channels on the tv knowing that nothing was going to catch my attention, but I didn't have anything else to do. I'd already done my homework for the week, studied as much as I could, and even cleaned up my house from the top to bottom. A ghost of a smile came across my face as I thought back over the last week; I spent the entire weekend getting to know CJ more. We laughed, joked, studied, and fucked like crazy, and my ass enjoyed every minute of it. When Sunday night came, neither of us wanted it to end, so we continued through the week; he took me to class every day and would pick me up when he didn't have his classes to attend. We fell into a smooth little routine of things, but I knew I needed to come home and give us a little space. I didn't want to get too comfortable with a man I was just getting to know and let my guard down as I did with Tika.

Boom. Boom. Boom

I looked up at my door and immediately got an attitude; only one person beat on my door like that. Getting up, I slowly walked to the door, taking my time because an unannounced visitor was not someone I was going to rush for. I snatched open the door to Red standing there with her arms crossed over her chest and smacking on her damn gum, looking like a cow chewing its cud.

I rolled my eyes at her and walked back to the living room, sitting on the couch. I waited for the lecture she thought she was about to give me.

"Bitch, where you been?" Red questioned as she stormed into the house. It took everything in me to school my features when she damn near jumped out her skin when she realized my bearded dragon Timber was out and sitting on my shoulder.

"I'm grown Red; I don't have to answer to you." I responded as I gently stroked Timber under her chin. Even though Red and I had been friends for years, I didn't owe her an explanation for anything that I did or where I decided to be at any given moment.

"I ain't seen your ass since we went to that club, one minute we were kicking it, and then guns were pulled and Tika was getting his life threaten by some nigga, and then you were gone." Red responded; she blatantly ignored my comment about not answering her. "Now Tika calling for a war with that nigga because he tried him in front of every-body and he saying he snatched you up and made you come with him."

"That ain't near what happened." I shook my head at her as I got up to put Timber back in her cage. "And please explain to me why Tika and the rest of the boys thought that party was a party for him and me getting back together? The last time I checked, Tika and I were not back together; in fact, we haven't spoken in months, and you told me that you got this club invite from Swiss."

38

"Girl, you know how Tika is." She said as she waved me off. Yeah, I knew how Tika was, but I also know how Red rocks when it comes to Tika. That party shit was planned, and she helped him out with getting me there. I let out a small laugh as I thought about it; both of their asses were playing right now, and I was not about to be put back in a situation where I looked like the fool.

"Red, stop playing with me." I responded as I walked into the kitchen to wash my hands. I could hear her suck her teeth at my comment. Shaking my head, I counted to ten in my head to help me control my temper.

"I'm serious! Tika just is trying to show you he for real about being a changed man and him throwing the party was just him being him." She let out a small laugh of her own at her comment; of course, Tika was just going to be Tika, but too many people had let him do what the hell he wanted for some long that he didn't know how to react when people told him no. "But anyway, my mama wants to see you at her cookout she got going, so go get dressed."

"Girl, what's with the last-minute invite?" I questioned as I grabbed a paper towel off the counter, dried my hands, and turned off the water.

"It's a last-minute thing all around." Red said with a shrug. "My brothers' plug got his hand on a meat truck the other day and they packed our houses up but we had so much leftover that my stepdad said he couldn't let it go to waste so they throwing a small little get together."

"I'm going to pass on this one; I got some studying to do." I said shaking my head. Even though I didn't, she didn't know that, and it wasn't her business if I did or not.

"Come on Dove." Red responded sucking her teeth. "All you do is study; you don't ever go out no more or spend time with me! You know how my mama can be too! As soon as I show up without you she gonna be calling you telling you to bring your ass, so you might as well come with me now, so you don't have to hear her loud ass mouth over the phone".

I stood leaning over the couch listening to her, she was right. Her mama would call me and pretty much guilt trip me into coming over if I didn't show. Plus, I haven't eaten all day and if her step daddy was doing his thing on the grill, I knew the food was going to be good as hell. Nodding, I raised from the couch and headed to my room. "Give me like thirty minutes to get showered and changed." I threw over my shoulder before closing the door.

Two hours later, I wanted to smack the shit out of Red; this was not the small little get together that she swore up and down it was going to be on the ride over. At first, I thought everything would be okay; there were people, mainly family, sitting around enjoying themselves. For the first thirty minutes or so, I enjoyed myself, even joined in on a few spades' games with Red's aunties. I ate some good ass food and even smoked a blunt or two. Then Red's mama asked us to make a store run to grab some more liquor and some shells for the weed. I knew the minute I got out of the car; it was about to be some shit; the entire neighborhood had shown up while we were gone. Kids were running around playing, and the music was so loud coming from the back yard that my head was starting to hurt. A few people had a dice game going, the old heads were playing spades and tunk now and a couple of basket-ball games were being played in the park that sat across the street.

"Oh, shit, look what the cat drug in, hey there, little birdy." Chester yelled from the driveway. Growing up, Uncle Chester had treated me like family and was one of the few people that didn't switch up when my mama went to jail. I think it was because he had a sweet spot for her and was heartbroken that she went down with her husband.

"Hey Chester, how you doing?" I said hugging him. I laughed as he rocked me back and forth before letting me go. Chester always had some words of wisdom to drop on you at just the right moment each time you saw him.

"Shit, you know how it is, baby girl, just making it one day at a time. How you been?" He responded then questioned in return. Chester wasn't a bad-looking man; he was short maybe five-four but was buff for no reason besides he stayed working out. He did a ten-year bid when he was in his early twenties, and when he was released, he continued his work out. His bald head stayed shinning, glasses, and a strong jawline; I always thought he looked like a short Ving Rhymes.

"Not too bad." I nodded as I looked around at everyone. More people were showing up, which meant it was getting closer to the time for me to leave.

"You still in school?" He questioned as he watched Tika make his way towards us. He was dressed in a pair of yellow shorts, a crisp white tee, and a pair of yellow and white Nike Shox's. The mug he had on his face let me know he was about to be on some shit.

"Yes, sir, I have a few months left, then I'm done for good." I nodded as I crossed my arms over my chest. I sucked my teeth in agitation when I realized why Red kept insisting that I wear white and yellow instead of the black and grey romper that I decided to wear instead. Rolling my eyes, I brought my attention back to Chester; Tika was not about to ruin my attitude with his piss poor one.

"Good. Don't let these niggas take your focus from that. You got a good head on your shoulders, and that nigga right there ain't with you growing as a woman and getting out the hood." Chester said nodding his head in Tika's direction before turning towards me. "Get yo ass out of this place; it's all yo mama wants for yall now." He always wanted better for us since he didn't have any kids of his own, so I know what he was telling me was not only my mama's words but his too.

"I know." I said, nodding; I smiled at the mention of my mama from Chester. He didn't tell too many people because he said no one needed to be in their business but them. But he stayed accepting her calls, going to see her and putting money on her books. The last time she and I spoke she told me that Chester even had a lawyer working on her case, she said something about my father never specifically said her name in his sworn statements, he only referred to her as his wife. Legally, my parents were never married which not too many people knew, so she hoped she could get out on that technicality.

"What's up, baby?" Tika said as he approached us; he bent in for a hug that I sidestepped. "Oh, it's like that still?" He let out a short laugh as I rolled my eyes at him. He always thought everything was a joke, this time was no different.

"I'll see you around Chester." I said, waving and giving him a small smile. Chester, in turn, did the same before walking away, neither acknowledging Tika with a hello or goodbye. I didn't even look back at Tika as he called my name, he knew exactly how I planned to handle him, and I didn't see the point of faking it. I rounded the house looking for Red, I was ready to go, and she drove me here. "I knew I should've driven my damn self." I mumbled to myself as I searched the backyard for her.

"Who you looking for Dove?" Riley, one of Red's little cousin, asked as she walked up to me with a baby on her hip. Riley was about sixteen and had a good head on her shoulders. She stayed out of trouble and didn't run behind any boys; her only problem was her mama Kiesha. Kiesha stayed in the streets running behind a different nigga every week and had a baby to try to keep one of them. When that didn't work Kiesha was back in the streets, and Riley was looking after a new baby that wasn't hers.

"Red, she drove me here and I'm ready to go." I said to Riley as I smiled at her baby sister.

"She went on another run for her mama, I think; she just pulled off not too long ago." Riley said, her eyes were on her other two little brothers as they wrestled not too far from us.

"Shit, thanks, Riley." I responded to her back as she went to break apart her siblings. Trying to not let my frustration show, I headed back to the front of the house. I tried to get control of my anger with each step I took, Red no good ass knew not to leave me here, especially if Tika was going to show up or if it was a possibility. Pulling out my phone, I stood near the cars so I could have some privacy.

"Hello?" Red said after having to call her more than three times.

"Why didn't you tell me you were leaving?" I questioned as I waved at the little kids as they crossed the street to play in the park.

"For what Dove? You ain't my man. I don't have to check in with you." Red said with an attitude; I pulled the phone from my face and stared at it for a second.

"Red, I rode with you. Had I known you were leaving; I would've asked you to drop me off at home on your way to the store." I said once I put the phone back to my ear.

"I went the opposite way from your house. Have Tika take you home." Red said.

"Red, you already know I'm not fucking with Tika like

that stop fucking playing." I responded with my attitude. Why she was pushing this Tika thing so hard was beyond me, mostly since she was the main one yelling fuck him when I left.

"Well, that ain't my fault!" She said as she sucked her teeth. "Look, I'm about to get out the car to make this run inside real quick; when I make my next run, if it's in your direction, I'll let you know so I can drop you off." With that, she hung up in my face. I knew she wasn't making a store run because of how she worded her shit; she was making a run for Tika.

I gripped my phone in my hand tightly as I tapped it against my forehead, I squeezed my eyes shut in an attempt to keep the tears that wanted to drop in. I wasn't crying because she left me or even hung up on me. I cried when my anger got the best of me, and it was the only way I could release it without going off on someone. Red had me completely fucked up if she thought I was about to ask Tika for anything. Opening my eyes, I let out a deep breath once I realized how much I was being played. I dialed another number, hoping like hell the person answered the phone.

"What's up?" CJ's deep voice greeted me, causing a shiver to run down my spine. Immediately my mind flashed back to all the things he did to my body when I was with him.

"CJ." I damn near mumbled to him.

"What's wrong, Dove?" He questioned, the playfulness that had been in his voice when he first answered was now gone.

"Can you come to pick me up?" I asked. "I came out knowing I shouldn't have, and now I need a ride home. If you're busy I can uber home."

"Drop me your location." He responded and hung up

the phone. I did what he said and waited. There was no reason for me to go back inside because I didn't bring anything besides my phone and purse that I never put down. While I waited, I played a word trivia game on my phone against my sister that she sent me a while back.

"Why you keep playing with me, Dove?" Tika questioned from behind me. Again, I didn't acknowledge him. Tika was like a starved dog when it came to attention; as soon as you patted him on his head, he would keep coming back, but as soon as he felt threatened, he would attack. "So, you just gonna keep ignoring me?"

"Tika, we don't have anything to talk about." I said, finally taking my eyes off my phone to look at him. Even though he pissed me off I couldn't deny how fine Tika was. He was a yellow pretty boy, he had green eyes, long curly hair he always wore in a man bun, perfectly white smile even though he had a gap, thick pink lips, and a babyface because for the life of him he couldn't grow facial hair to save his life. I used to tease him, saying that he couldn't grow it because he refused to eat pussy and all the niggas with thick beards had their shit moisturized with pussy juice.

"Nah we don't Tika." I said shaking my head. "You did what you did and didn't think you would get caught but you did."

"How many times I gotta tell you I'm sorry for that shit? I was just trying to get that shit out of my system before we said our vows." Tika said as he tried to grab my hand. I stepped back as I snatched my hand away again; this nigga just didn't understand the word no. Now I didn't want to embarrass him, but if he kept it up, I would let him know a few things.

"Tika, just let it go. We good, we not together but we good." I said shaking my head. My heart began to beat wildly in my chest as his face tightened in anger; Tika was known to let his temper flare at any given moment.

"Dove, you starting to piss me off." Tika said as he grabbed the front of my romper and pulled me closer to him. This was the problem with the hood, shit like this was normal to them, so no one saw him grabbing me up as an issue. "I ain't forgot about ole' boy pulling that gun out on me at the club; I'm just letting that shit slide for now cause I got other shit in the works for him."

"Let me go Tika." I said as I tried to pry his hands away from my clothes.

"Nah you gonna listen to me and stop trying to play me like a fuck nigga. You already know how I get down Dove; I'll kill you and that nigga before I let him have you." Tika said. I knew for a fact he wasn't lying; he would rather kill me than look like he lost me to someone else.

5

Cj

"GPS says she should be over there." Benny said as he pulled up on the curb. The minute Dove dropped me her location and realized where she was, I called up Benny, and he and the boys followed me out. I had some people put some feelers out to find out what I could about Dove's ex Tika, and from what I could find out, he was the type of nigga I didn't fuck with. Tika was a local dope boy that was starting to make a name for himself over the last few years. Niggas didn't fear nor respect him but because he stayed with the good product that sold and had feens coming back for more people dealt with him. "Aye, CJ, there she goes right there, and it looks like that nigga got his hands on her!"

Without thinking or caring, I got out of the car. I knew Benny and the boys were right behind me, but it didn't matter because that nigga Tika just signed his death certificate by putting his hands on Dove. I pulled up my black shorts and turned my fit around backward so they could see my eyes. I wanted them niggas to see what death looked like.

"Nigga, take your fucking hands off my woman!" I said as I stepped onto the grass and pulled Dove from his grips. I positioned her behind me as I got into Tika's face. I wanted this nigga to say the wrong thing because my trigger finger was burning to be squeezed.

"Nigga yo woman?! I broke that bitch in and taught her the game how she yo woman huh?" Tika said, stepping into my face. He was so close to me that if he breathed too hard his spit could fall onto my face. "I taught her to suck dick and throw that pussy back. I had her screaming my name out when her mama was being thrown into the Feds. It was my seed she was swallowing for the last five years but you want to claim her as yours?" He shook his head, laughing as he stepped back two steps.

"My nigga you talking about little boy shit! You started fucking with her when she was young in the brain. That one right there?" I said, pointing to Dove, who was still positioned behind me with her arms wrapped around my waist. Gently she called my name as she pulled me away from Tika. "That grown-ass woman that she is right now? That's all me. You and everybody around this bitch better understand me. I'll air this bitch out about that one, don't try to play around and find out."

"Little nigga don't nobody fear you around this mutha-fucka!" Tika said as he raised his hands, looking around. He waited for someone to back what he was saying. It was a few of his boys that pulled me back, even though they didn't say anything I knew without a doubt that didn't agree with his statement. They knew who I was around here; they knew what the fuck I was about and who raised me. It seemed like this nigga was the only one who didn't know and was begging to find out. "I run this shit! I'm the king of this shit!"

"CJ come on. He's not worth it." Dove said as she pulled me further away from him. Benny and my boys stood at her side, waiting on my cue to let the bullets fly. The adults were smart enough to get the kids out the way and behind the house because if anything happens, we all know bullets don't have a name to them, and kids were off-limits.

"Don't get yourself handled, playboy. That's the second time you've disrespected her, don't let it be a third or your people will be putting flowers on your fucking headstone." I said; at that threat, Dove stepped in front of me. If I weren't in such a bad mood, I'd laugh at her little ass trying to step in front of me. Why women thought they could stop their nigga by doing that shit was beyond me, but at the same time, I understood the need to protect what's yours.

"Can we go, please?" She said, grabbing my face so that I could look at her. She knew my attention needed to be fully on her or I'd make good on my promise and end Tika right then and there. "CJ baby, I want to go; take me home, please." I stared down at her and realized something; Dove never acknowledged him, never said a word, or took her attention off of me even for a second. She even turned her back to him, an ultimate sign of disrespect in the hood. You never gave your back to the person until you had nothing to fear and did not respect that person. "I want to go home, get in the bed, and lay up under you like we did before. But baby, I can't do that by myself; I need you to lay with me, laugh with me, smile with me, joke with me."

Without a word, I nodded my head, Dove, and pulled her close to me to kiss her. At that moment it was either kiss her or kill that nigga. And even though I wanted to body this nigga with everything in me, I refused to put her in harm's way to prove my point. I was better than that, and if my grandmother found out I put Dove in harm's, she'd come after me her damn self, and I couldn't have that. Once I was satisfied with my kiss, I pulled away, and we headed to the car; the entire time, Tika's stupid ass was jaw-jacking to the people who would listen. Nigga didn't even know the next party he'd be at would be his funeral.

"What the fuck was you doing with that nigga Dove?" I questioned as I pulled off from the curb. I quickly glanced over at Dove as I turned the corner. She sat there looking at her nails, her face tore up with frustration and anger, but she wasn't pouting. If anything, she seemed more pissed off than I was.

"Red came over and said her mama was throwing a small get-together and wanted me to come with her." Dove said.

"That's the same nigga from the club, ain't it?" I questioned as I turned the corner; at this point, I was just driving, with no real destination in mind. I wasn't taking her back with me to the trap house, and I wasn't due to be back at the club for another few hours.

"Yeah." She said, her attention now on the front windshield but I could tell she wasn't paying attention to that shit either.

"Them niggas don't sit right with me; stop fucking with them." I said as I turned into my favorite little hole in the wall BBQ spot. The line wasn't long, and it wouldn't have mattered if it were cause I never stood in that shit. I knew the owner, and I knew the second my truck hit the parking lot that someone would start making my normal order. "Benny, don't go in there fucking with Carter; you know she not gonna be in the mood for your shit." I handed Benny more than enough to cover all three of our meals, plus leave a nice tip. Benny smiled and nodded his head as he got out of the car. I chuckled as my nigga made his way inside; he would piss off Carter just because he could. "I'm serious, Dove, that nigga not right in the head."

"I hear you." She said.

"I know what you heard, Dove, but I'm asking you, do you understand what I'm saying?" Gently, I turned her face so that she could see how serious I was. "I'm not the type of nigga to drop what I'm doing to come and rescue somebody who's gonna keep going back to the same situation. As much as I enjoy rocking with you, I will let your ass back out on that corner and let that nigga hem you up some more, and when he finally snaps and kill you, I'll drop flowers on your grave a few times, and that's it."

"I said I heard you." She said nodding her head, she gave me that damn puppy dog look females give they nigga when they know they in trouble and I laughed. I pulled her into another kiss, this one quicker, and then settled back into my seat, waiting on Benny to show his face. I let out another laugh when my phone started to ring; I knew without looking over that it was Carter calling to complain about Benny.

"Say what you need, big cousin." I said laughing after I hit the green button to answer the call.

"Why the fuck do you send this nigga in here every time?" Carter questioned; I could hear her typing away at her computer. "He comes in here, loud as hell, causing problems, and then strolls out this bitch like he the owner and it say his name on the marquee outside."

"My shit could be out there if you stop playing; we change that name from Carter's BBQ to B&C BBQ." Benny said, laughing; I knew he was standing in the door frame of her office, giving her a hard time because that's what he'd done since I introduced them a few years back.

"All you gotta do is stop playing and let a nigga wife you up, drop a few kids in you and I'll take care of you."

"Benny, I will call Parker and Emanuel if you don't get the fuck out of my building." Carter threatened him, I knew they were going to argue for a few minutes, so I hung up the phone. Leaning back in my seat, I turned my head to look over at Dove. We sat in silence while we waited for Benny; she was lost in her thoughts, and me just content with watching her. About ten minutes later, Benny came out of the restaurant with a big ass smile on his face.

"Here, man, she said your money isn't welcomed in her establishment any longer." Benny said, handing me my money back; we ended up at Dove's spot since it was closer to the club and knew if I went home, I wouldn't have wanted to leave.

"Man, you gonna end up with a bullet in your ass if you keep messing with that girl." I said, laughing as I took my money back, easing back on the couch; I pulled a sleeping Dove closer to me and let her relax.

"Carter just gotta stop acting like she doesn't want me; I already know she does." Benny said with a shrug as he cleaned up his mess. Even though Benny and I had grown up together and Carter was my cousin, they didn't cross paths until a few years ago. Mainly because Carter grew up on the good side of town, her daddy, who was my uncle, didn't want her mixed up in the shit he was involved with, so he set her and her mama up there and didn't let her come around often. She went off to college, got her degree, and was living her life until about seven years ago. She got mixed up with the wrong nigga who was beating her ass and damn near killed her, and it was the life her pops didn't want her involved in that saved her ass. That and her cousin Parker on her mama side of the family. Parker and her mama Parish came out the blue one night at the hospital, didn't say too many words, just saw how Carter was, and it was like a switch was flipped in them. Carter mama Candace didn't even say shit, just hugged her sister and niece, and they rolled out. A few days later they found his body hanging off his balcony by his bowels. When Carter woke up and found out what happened she didn't even question who did it or why, she knew the moment Parker walked into the room to visit her.

"She threatened you with Parker and her crazy ass husband this time, though." I said with a laugh. I felt Dove look up at me; looking down, I smiled at her; I could tell she had questions about what we were talking about. "Carter has a cousin on her mama side who is a killer, and when shit gets rough for Carter, she will call her, and then bodies will start dropping."

"We all got killers in our family though." Dove shrugged as if it was no big deal. It's crazy how much the streets change people. Here we are talking about death and killing people like it was an everyday occurrence, and for us, it was. We dealt with death no matter the circumstances of it like it was a trip to the store. It was something that the hood lived through with ease while the rest of society turned their noses down on us. Yeah, we had an issue, and I was one of the first ones to admit it, but no one wanted to admit that we survived the best way that we could. The lack of education and resources would always be a major issue. The rest of the world thought if a few of us could make it out, that meant that we all were supposed to. They thought a few ballplayers and rappers spoke for all of us.

"True but not like her baby girl is an assassin, like was trained for this shit. She mad cool, though, can come into any room and be the life of the party. Clowning and every-thing even got a regular job and shit." Benny said, walking back into the room. "But when she about to do something? Nah, I don't know a nigga that could fuck with her."

"What about her husband?" Dove questioned as she sat up in her seat.

"That nigga crazier than she is!" I said, laughing; pulling out my bag of weed, I started to break it down. Glancing over, I watched as my phone lit up with a text from a few of my boys; it looked like this nigga Tika was still making noise. Talking about how he was going to have to check me over his bitch and then put a bullet in both of us for running around behind his back.

"Nigga is crazy, like murder turn that nigga on or something cause they are fucking after it like he took her on a romantic date or something," Benny said, laughing as he broke his weed. "They a killer couple, literally."

"Right." I agreed; picking up my phone, I sent a message to my boy Ezell, letting him know I would be meeting up with him later tonight. "I'm surprised they don't have a bunch of kids running through here."

"Nigga even the kids would be killers!" Benny said laughing.

"They can't be that bad." Dove said as she pulled her books from her bag, shit was sexy as hell. She stayed in the books; it didn't matter what we were doing or who was around. The entire weekend she was at my house, they were open, and if I wanted her attention, she gave it to me but always went back to her books. "Now, do you want Carter like you say you do, or is it just easy to mess with her since she doesn't want to deal with you like that?"

"Benny knows he ain't the type of nigga Carter needs to deal with." I said, agreeing with Dove's point of view. As much as I loved my cousin, she didn't belong with a street nigga, and that's exactly what Benny was right now. He had the potential to be more, but he wasn't ready to let the bitches go, and I was cool with that. He told me straight out that he wouldn't step to her right now, and when he was ready, if he ever were, he would treat her like she deserved. He didn't want her to wait for him though, he told her if she found someone who could do everything, he couldn't that he wouldn't object to it.

"Nah, I ain't what she needs." Benny said shaking his head. I could tell he wanted to say more but something was stopping him from saying it aloud. "What are you studying?" Benny asked as he lit up his blunt. The entire conversation about Parker was long forgotten. No lie, I was kind of relieved about it. Not too many people knew what Parker did, and I didn't want to hear Carter's mouth later about her crazy-ass cousin.

"The same thing he is." Dove pointed over to me without looking up. If she had she would've seen the confused look on Benny's face. She took her favorite pen and stuck it in her top bun; no matter how many times she did this, in a few minutes, she would be looking for it.

"Ugh, Dove that nigga ain't never had a book about zoo's out that I've ever seen," Benny said as he picked up one of her books that sat on her table. I chuckled as I took a pull from my blunt and sat back on the couch next to Dove.

"What?" Dove said, looking up from her book; she stared at Benny for a few seconds, then looked over at me. "Why are you in my class?" Her dark eyes lit up with excitement; it was like something so simple as a man pursuing her was something new to her.

"Shit, I wanted to get to know you." I responded with a shrug. Even though I seemed calm on the outside I was really about to start sweating bullets. This nigga Benny was running his damn mouth because he knew I couldn't deny shit that he said. "I saw you a few times on campus and saw you walk into Professor White's class; he is one of my plugs, so he ain't say shit to me about being there. After a while, I started enjoying the shit; I'm not officially in the class, but I do the work, and Professor Glass punk-ass even grades it just for the hell of it."

"Wait, hold on." Dove responded with a laugh, she sat up in her seat to get a better look at me. "You're telling me that you sit in a grad level class and do the work because you wanted to get to know me? When all you had to do was ask me for my number instead of doing all that extra?" She asked with a smile on her face. I knew without a doubt that she was going to clown my ass later for it, but I don't care.

"Didn't I tell you a while back that I could see myself rocking with you?" I questioned; I waited for her to think back to our conversation. She nodded after a few seconds. "I wasn't playing."

"I could've been the opp for all you know." She said laughing. Instead of responding, I pushed her books closer to her and took another pull of my blunt. This damn girl was crazy as hell.

Dove

"I BEEN TOLD you to stop fucking with that bitch Red, but you didn't want to listen." My sister Lily said as she turned the corner, we were heading to our Aunt Constance's house for Sunday dinner. We hadn't spoken for a few days and was using this time to catch up on each other's lives. "I told you when I met that hoe that she was envious of you."

"This doesn't have nothing to do with Red though Lily; this was all Tika doing." I said as I scrolled through my text with CJ. We spent the rest of the day together yesterday before he and Benny had to make a few runs. He wanted me to stay at his house last night just to be safe, but I just wanted to study in my bed, then take a bubble bath and go to sleep. He pouted for a few minutes, but then Benny told him they needed to go, and they left; it didn't stop him from texting me all night and even sending me a few pictures of his dick, saying that it missed me too.

"Girl, you crazy in your fucking head if you think for one minute that she ain't have nothing to do with it." Lily said as she pulled into the driveway. Aunt Constance sat on the porch steps watching as her two big ass Dobermans ran around her yard. "That bitch right in his ear telling him everything you are doing, and that's only if she ain't sucking his dick. Talking about that's her play brother. I have yet to see a bitch that close to her play brother without them having something going on. That's why I don't believe a bitch when she calls a nigga her bestie. Yeah, they besties alright, the best at sucking and fucking each other on the low."

"They grew up together." I responded as we got out of the car in response to her comment about them possibly having a sexual relationship. Lily never liked Red and always voiced her opinion about it if she was brought up. More times than not, I kept them apart because Lily didn't give any fucks about telling Red about herself, and Red knew how I got down. If she jumped stupidly at my sister, I was going to take her fucking head off. I waved to our aunt as I rounded the car. Growing up, I used to think that Lily was Constance's daughter because they favored so much; they were the color of honey and stood a few inches taller than me but didn't have my shape. They were skinny, with small titties, round faces, big ass eyes, and lips with a short pudgy nose. Constance was old school and had gold on her front tooth, and Lily wore silver fangs. My entire life Constance always wore locs and about three years ago Lily loc'd her hair up too.

"I don't give a damn; they didn't pop out the same pussy or dick, so they ain't related." Lily said as she rolled her eyes. She approached our aunt first and hugged her with me following right behind her. "Auntie, tell your niece that Tika and Red got something going on."

"I have to agree with Lily on this one." Was all Constance said as she stepped back, her face was twisted like she smelled something foul. "They ain't right."

"Why didn't nobody think to say something before?" I questioned as we followed her inside the house. We made our way through to the kitchen, where Constance had enough food sitting around to feed a small army instead of just the three of us. Like the little kids that we were when it came to her and our mom we stood in line and waited to wash our hands.

"Girl you were too much in love with that yellow nigga to tell you anything. We couldn't tell you shit about Tika and you know it." Constance said as she finished washing her hands so that she could prepare our plates. It was then that I noticed she had a lot of food already in to-go plates. "And yes, before you ask, the rest is for yall to take home with yall. I already know between studying and work, yall don't have no time to cook shit for the next few days."

Behind her back, Lily and I started to twerk; even though Lily didn't have that much ass to shake, she did her best to keep up with me. I threw my hand in the air as I dropped it to the floor which caused Lily to start laugh and caused Constance to look over her shoulder to see what we were doing. She rolled her eyes and went back to making our plates, we were grown, and she was used to dealing with our antics. Constance stayed hooking us up with food, and we were always grateful for it and her. Since our mama, her sister, had been locked up, she'd stepped up, even more, making sure we didn't need anything, and if we did, she made sure we had it. She always told us that our mama didn't need to worry about what we were doing or if we were being looked after because she was around. She had her sister back just like I had mine.

"Speaking of Tika, I heard about the BBQ." Constance said as she handed us our plates and began to make her own. "Do I need to send your cousins over to have a word with him or does that new boy that came to your rescue have it all under control?"

"What new boy?!" Lily questioned as she sat down; her big eyes were wide with surprise as she looked at me. "Are you telling me, big sister, that it's someone else sniffing behind you, and you ain't say nothing the entire car ride over here?"

"How did you find out?" I asked Constance instead of answering Lily as I took my seat next to Lily. She said a quick prayer over our food before taking a bit, she didn't respond. Instead, she gave me a sneaky smile and shrugged her shoulders. "Oh, so you gonna just play me like that and not tell me who running they mouth about my business?"

"Yo, mama told me when I talked to her this morning." Constance said both Lily and my mouth dropped open in surprise. My mama wasn't even home and knew something? I knew when I went to see her next weekend that she was going to clown my ass.

"Who told her?" Lily asked as she laughed.

"You know Rose ain't telling who told her shit." Constance said as she cut into her cornbread. "My sister still got her hands in yall shit, protecting yall, even though she locked up. Now eat your food and tell me how school is going."

"It was probably Chester's ass; he always had a thing for mama." Lily said offhandedly as she picked up her phone. "That nigga overprotective like he our daddy more than that nigga who signed our birth certificate was."

"Respect that man; he goes hard for your mama always treated her like she was a queen. Give him respect for that alone." Constance said. She pointed her fork at Lily and me before turning her attention back to her food. She didn't think I saw the smirk on her face, but I did. The smirk on her face told me she knew a lot more than what she was saying.

We sat around, talking, and eating for a few hours before Lily and I packed up and left. I had a long week with classes, and Lily had a packed schedule as well. We promised to call and let Constance know we were home and safe and we headed out. The drive home was smooth; we ended up taking a detour and meeting up with Lily's best friend Tatum before she hit the stage. Because we came to support her so often the bouncer at the door let us in even though we are in some leggings and tennis shoes which was against the dress code. We made our way to the bar, ordered a few drinks, and found a seat near the stage.

"Tay said she's been working on this new routine and was going to do it tonight." Lily said as she took a sip of her drink. Tatum and Lily had been friends since they were in elementary school, getting in trouble for fighting other little girls cause, at the time, Tatum had a stutter. Lily didn't and still doesn't like people being bullied and took it personally when she found out Tatum was having problems. When their teacher paired them up because unknown to anyone at the time, she had dyslexia and was behind on her reading skill they formed a tight bond and have been inseparable ever since.

"That's why it's so many people in here then?" I said, looking around at the packed club; Tatum was always known to draw a crowd when she danced. Over the last few months, she'd started taking the back seat and teaching the other girls instead of being on the stage. She taught them routines that she came up with and they paid her well for it. More often than not, she was booked out for at least six to eight weeks in advance, so if she was on the stage, it meant that she wanted to be and didn't need to be.

"You already know how my girl gets down." Lily said with a smile. I smiled at the pride she had for her friend. A lot of times, people, especially our people, acted as if it hurt them to support their friends. But not Lily; she told any and everyone that her best friend was the hottest dancer in KC and meant that shit from the heart. "Plus, the word is that nigga Focus is gonna be in here, and I want to see what he looks like."

"What the fuck you gonna do with a rapper Lily? You don't even listen to the shit." I questioned; she looked at me for a second and burst into laughter. It was true; as ghetto as my sister was, she didn't listen to rap unless she was with Tatum or me. Any other time it was blasting that 80's and 90's R&B, she said rap made her head hurt. So, her being interested in a rapper was comical.

"I will learn some lyrics if he fine enough." Lily said with a shrug, sad part about it was I knew my sister was serious as hell. Before I could respond, the lights dropped lower, and the DJ Life voice bounced over the entire room.

"Alright, I know why yall here! Yall heard my girl was coming to the stage, and y'all wanted to see the hottest dancer in the Midwest show us what she got, huh?" Life yelled into the microphone; the crowd instantly perked up. Don't get me wrong, the chicks that just came off the stage were doing their thing, but tonight's crowd was all about Tatum. "Everybody knows the rules when Tatum takes the stage; the entire city shuts down! Get your hundreds ready cause that's what she deserves! So, without further due, coming to the stage is the one and only Tatum!"

As soon as Life finished his speech, he dropped the lights, shinning the spotlight on the center pole. Even before she stepped onto the stage money was being thrown on it, fifty, twenty and hundreds ran down on the floor, I knew without a doubt that Tatum would be cashing in major tonight.

"Let's go bestie!" Lily yelled as Tatum gracefully walked to the stage; her dark skin glistened; no doubt she'd oiled up right before hitting the stage. In one smooth motion, Tatum dropped down in a split and bounced her ass, giving everyone a peek of her rhinestone g string panties that she wore. When the beat dropped again, and her favorite song by Janet Jackson called Would You Mind came on, I knew this was about to get interested. I sat back in my seat and prepared to enjoy the show.

"That girl probably got three niggas in here pregnant." I said to Lilly as we made our way to the door. Tatum's show was wild and sexual in a way that most strippers didn't try to do. Most used loud music with a heavy baseline, while Tatum usually used slower songs with a smooth, mellow beat.

"Had them sitting around with their mouth stuck

open." Lily said laughing, we weaved through the crowd, trying to get out of the building before the crowd started to make their way out too. "But I can't even lie. She made me want to learn some of the moves she did."

"Right, but what I don't want to do is fall and bust my damn head open cause I'm not as coordinated as she is. My big ass would get on that pole and slid right the fuck back down and split my head open." I said, stepping on the sideway, luckily, we didn't park far, and it wasn't too dark in the parking lot.

We linked arms as we made our way towards the car, scanning the parking lot as we walked. It was too quiet of a night for someone not to be making some noise about something, and knowing the niggas around here, they were waiting for the right or wrong reason to show their asses.

"You damn sure would and I'd be right on the front row taping that shit and yelling *World Star!*" Lily said as she unlocked the doors and we climbed into her 2020 burnt orange hellcat charger.

"Damn you'd play me like that?" I questioned as I put on my seat belt.

"Have we met?" Lily responded. We sat staring at each other for a few seconds before we burst into laughter. After getting herself together Lily wiped the tears from her eye and pulled off. We rode home, not talking; Toni Braxton played in the background with each of us lost in our thoughts.

"Ugh, it's somebody parked in your driveway." Lily said as she pulled in, blocking whoever's it was in. "If it's that nigga Tika, I'm popping my trunk."

I laughed at her comment but stayed in my seat, watching as the driver and passenger door of the black truck opened. A smile spread across my face once I realized it was CJ and Benny getting out.

63

"Oh, that's the nigga Auntie was talking about huh?" Lily questioned as I rolled my window down. "Aye, what are you doing in my sister's driveway like you, her man?" Lily yelled as soon as CJ bent down to look into the window. He smiled at her but didn't reply; instead, he looked over at me and winked.

"She is mine," CJ said, never taking his eyes off me; if I were light skin, he would be able to tell that I was blushing. I could tell he'd been drinking; his eyes were low and slightly red. He didn't smell like weed, so I knew he wasn't high. But he looked and smelled good, he wore a pair of black cargo shorts, a red chiefs jersey, a red KC hat, and a pair of black and red custom Chiefs chucks I know he paid a ridiculous amount of money for because I saw them online a few weeks ago and the starting price was $275.

"She ain't tell me that," Lily said, watching CJ. When he looked up at her he laughed and shook his head. "Lily why you always giving me a hard time? When I see you with Tatum and now when you with my woman? I ain't ever did shit to you."

"Cause you always talking shit whenever I see you," Lily said; she pressed the button to roll up my window and looked over at me. "CJ is a big ass upgrade from Tika." Instead of waiting for me to reply, she hopped out of the car; I could hear her talking shit to Benny as soon as her head cleared the door.

"I didn't realize Lily was your sister," CJ said after he opened my door, he reached in and helped me out of the car. I looked over and immediately shook my head at Lily who was now on Benny's back. Her laughter only drowned out her screams as he ran around the front yard with her on his back.

"Oh, you ain't question Lily's loyalty like you did mine?" I questioned as I leaned against her car, crossing my arms over my chest; I looked up at CJ with a smirk on my face. He ran his hands down his face and sucked his teeth at me before he looked down at me.

"I ain't question your loyalty to the world; I just needed to know that if it went down, who head you'd be holding that nine against? Mine or that nigga Tika's." CJ said as he looked down at me. That was something I was starting to notice about him. His eyes were always on me; whenever he talked to me, he gave me his full attention. Tika never did that.

"You think you know the answer to that already?" I questioned; I crossed my arms over my chest and leaned back against the car.

"I know it, ain't no thinking about it." CJ said as he bent down, he grazed my ear with his teeth before planting a kiss behind it. "The second you told me you trusted me while you were riding in that passenger seat told me every-thing I needed to know."

"You cocky as hell, you know that?" I questioned with a laugh. I didn't have a rebuttal for what he said because it was the truth. He didn't have to question it because my word was all I had, and I'd given it to him and only him.

"Nah baby it ain't about being cocky, it's about being solid in where I stand. I know you a real one, and you being Lily's big sister and your mama being Rose just pushed you to a higher level." CJ said as he pulled back. "Yo baby sister a real one just like yo mama and you."

"Yeah, baby sis, not about the games. As much of a dork as she is, she rolls hard for the ones she considers hers." I said, nodding in agreement. I looked back to see that she and Benny were now sitting on the porch talking. He dwarfed her in size, but they looked good together. "How long have you known her?"

"Man, I been rocking it with Lily for as long as Tatum

been at the club, they a package deal that causes problems wherever they go." CJ said with a shrug. "She always told me she had a sister that stayed with her head in the books; I just didn't put two and two together. Yall don't look nothing alike."

"She looks like our auntie; I look like my mama." I replied with a shrug.

"Okay, I can see that." CJ nodded his head; he looked over at Lily again, then back at me as he put a toothpick in his mouth. "She got a hell of a temper on her, though; I had to cancel a few of the hits she had on yall pops head when all that shit happened."

"She said if she sees's him, she's putting a bullet in that nigga head herself." I said, I allowed CJ to pull me close to his body and wrap his arms around me.

"I believe it." CJ responded as he rested his chin on my head. "She all Benny talks about. They kick it hard every week, but he knows that she deserves to get out of the hood, yeah she one of the hottest nail techs in KC; folks travel to see her; she does all the sports team's women's nails. She got a name for herself, and so does he but he a street nigga. He gotta look over his shoulder too much and would tear this entire thing down if something happens to her."

"What about Carter, though?" I asked; I didn't want my sister playing second fiddle to anyone, and yeah, Carter was CJ's family, but Lily is mine, and my loyalty goes to her first.

"Carter crazy ass is the one who pointed it out to him. Like I said, Lily and Benny hang out all the time, and she even knows Carter. That's why she never wanted anything to do with him like that cause she knows that he only messed with her because she and Lily are so much alike. She told that nigga today to go find Lily and make that shit official." CJ said, then placed a kiss on my head and pulled back. "He gonna treat your sister right, maybe she can even get him to step out the street life like I am trying to do."

"You trying to go on the straight and narrow?" I questioned in surprise, yeah I know he's in school and is doing big things in that, but from what I found out about CJ over the last few weeks, he was a street nigga to the fullest. He demanded respect from anyone who came in contact with him and dared someone to try him because he was known to pull the trigger without a second thought.

"Something like that." He responded as he pulled his phone out of his pocket. I watched as different emotions ran across his face before finally, he stood there with a blank look on his face. "Aye, grab yo shit, and let's go." He didn't give me a chance to respond before grabbing me by the hand and pulling me towards my front door.

"What's going down?" Benny questioned as he stood up; he could tell from the look on CJ's face that something was going on.

"She is grabbing some clothes and shit and going to my spot, this nigga Tika just shot up Ezell's spot, and word is he can't keep his mouth shut and is bragging about it." CJ said as he passed by Benny and Lily so that we could go into the house. I headed to my room while CJ stood back and talked to Benny. I didn't even think twice about what he said as I packed my clothes, throwing a few weeks' worths of things in a duffle bag, as well as my school bag and my travel case for Timber. Who knew if or when I was coming back, and I refused to leave her behind.

"Alright, I'm ready." I said, coming out of my room; CJ grabbed my duffle bag and backpack and handed them to Benny while I held on tight to Timber's case. I locked up my house then jumped into my truck; I followed behind

Benny and CJ with Lily right behind me. I said a small prayer as I drove; Tika had declared with a man who's revenge held no bounds, and even though he'd said earlier, he was trying to get out the streets, he wasn't out yet. If he felt like he was disrespected or being tried, he would show his ass.

6

Cj

"Man get your ass over here and stop playing." I said to Dove as I slid my dick back into her pussy. She let out a small whimper as I moved in and out of her. I grabbed her shoulder and pushed her further down on the bed; her arch was the best I'd ever seen, but I was trying to hit my favorite spot, and she kept moving. Talking some weak shit about it was too much for her to handle, but that was her fault; she came out the bathroom in some little ass shorts, a white beater with no bra, and sat down Indian style in the bed, so I couldn't help but see her fat ass pussy imprint. Immediately my dick got hard seeing that shit, then I remembered how it felt wrapped around my shit, and I was ready to fuck. But I tried to get her to change, even told her to have something different on by the time I got out of the shower but she didn't listen, it ain't my fault she had her headphones on and couldn't hear me. So when I got out of the shower, and she was still sitting there, I pulled her legs open, slid them bitches to the side, and licked her pussy like it was a hot summer day and she was a cold popsicle right out the freezer.

"Sss. CJ, wait." She attempted to push me away again, and just like last time, I grabbed hold of her wrist and pinned them to her back. I stroked her a few times, making her leg start to shake, and her pussy grip my dick even tighter, and I pulled out.

"The fuck?" She questioned, looking over her shoulder. Her eyes were glassy from pleasure. "Why did you stop?"

"You trust me?" I questioned as I stroked myself. I watched as her eyes dropped down to my dick, then back up to my face, and she nodded her head. I hopped off the bed and walked around to the dresser; it took me no time to find my ties and grabbing four. I looked over my shoulder to see Dove now sitting up in the bed watching me. I flashed her the ties and smiled at her. "Would you let me tie you up? I swear I won't do anything to hurt you." I didn't wait for her to respond as I made my way back over to the bed and climbed back in. Instinctively she laid back; I positioned myself in between her legs; my dick kept sliding against the crease of her pussy, it took everything in me not to slide back in, but I focused on tying up her wrist to the headboard.

"You did this before?" She questioned as I moved to her other hand.

"Nah, I wanted to but never asked a female to do it before." I replied with a shake of my head. Once her arms were secured, I went to work on her ankles. I climbed off the bed to make sure I tied her down correctly and didn't have it too tight to where the restraints would hurt her.

"So, this your first time?" Dove asked with a laugh, she even tried to make her voice sound deep so that she could mimic how niggas sounded when they first started messing with girls and was getting pussy for the first time. I looked up at her and shook my head again. "You trying to be nasty with me?" She always found a way to make me laugh or smile.

"Nah, I don't usually do this." I replied giving her the weak-ass line females like giving niggas when they let them hit after a short time of knowing them. Once her ankles were tied, I stepped back and admired Dove. She laid there, spread eagle with her bottom lip in between her teeth.

"You just standing there, my pussy gonna be dry by the time you get back in the bed." Dove said, her eyes dropped down to my dick, causing it to jump.

"I doubt that." I said as I stroked myself; I watched as her pussy juices dripped from her and puddled onto the sheet under her. I climbed back in the bed and kissed my way up her body; I pulled her nipple into my mouth and sucked on it, causing her to shiver and her other nipple to harden under my hand. I let go of her nipple and positioned my dick right at the crease of her pussy. I looked down at her as I slid back in; her mouth dropped open, and her eyes rolled in the back of her head. I started slow, allowing her body to readjust to me before I started pounding into her. Angling my hips down, I pushed harder into her; with each stroke, I circled my hips to make sure I brushed against her clit.

"Untie me." Dove said as she strained and pulled against the ties that we wrapped around her wrist. Her back arched off the bed but she couldn't go anywhere because she was tied down. "Shit CJ untie me." Our bodies smacked against each other; Dove probably had the wettest pussy I'd ever had because we sounded like we were mixing up five different bowls of mac and cheese. Each time I stroked her pussy, her eyes rolled further into the back of her head. I could feel her pussy tighten up on me and I went a little bit faster hoping to get her to nut, but she refused to let it go.

"Nah, don't try to hold it back, give me my nut Dove." I said as I reached back and untied her ankles without coming out of her. She didn't miss a beat; as soon as she realized her ankles were free, she wrapped them around my waist, and I fell deeper into her pussy.

"Untie my hands, and I will!" She practically cried as she pushed the lower half of her body to meet mine. I smirked at her request and moved my hips the other way; I knew that with the curve of my dick, I was hitting her favorite spot; her pussy clamping down tighter on my dick proved my point.

"Nah, give it to me now." I said before kissing her. She shook her head in refusal as I pulled back. "Come on girl! Just give it to me." She shook her head again, but this time, it was more of a jerky motion as she tried to control her nut. "Alright then since you playing, I'm taking two now." I bite down on her bottom lip and grabbed her hips. I grabbed a pillow that was pushed against the headboard and pushed them under her hips to angle her pussy up.

"Okay okay." Dove said as I tugged on her clit that was sticking straight up. She pulled against the ties again, but this time, she was using them as leverage so that she could pull away from me. "Shit CJ!"

I didn't respond as I grabbed tighter on her waist and pumped into her. Her pussy gripped my shit so hard I had to look down at Dove to make she didn't do it on purpose. From the way, her eyes fluttered behind her eyelids, and her mouth was open. I could tell she didn't. I went to work then, pushing up inside her as hard as I could but being cautious enough not to hurt her.

"Shit!" Dove yelled as she finally let go of the nut, she wasn't trying to let me have it, and again, she squirted all over me. I kept on moving, using her nut as extra lube as I chased behind my nut. It must've felt extra good to her because as soon as she finished one nut, another followed right behind it. I released my nut inside her and dropped my head down, my heart was beating fast as hell. I could feel her pussy tighten up and relax around my dick, but I couldn't make myself slid out of her.

"I'm gonna get you a towel; then I'll come and untie your wrist." I said, raising my head; I let out a small laugh when my eyes landed on Dove, who was fast asleep. Finally, I slid from her and made my way to the bathroom. Quickly I cleaned myself up with a warm towel and came back to the room to untie and clean her up. I grabbed a pair of boxer briefs and basketball shorts from my dresser and threw them on. I softly closed the door on my way out of the room and went into the living room. We hadn't been back at my place long before we ended up fucking, so her duffle bag and container that she had Timber in were both sitting on my dining room table. I grabbed a blunt I had sitting on the table on my way to the garage to get the extra tank I had stored in there.

With the phone connected to my sound system, I turned the volume low as I sat up Timber in the extra tank that I had. I lucked up because I still had all the extra supplies left over from when I upgraded my iguana's cage. After getting her all set up, I went to work on the kitchen, cleaning out the fridge and pulling out some meat from the freezer that I could cook tomorrow. Once everything was done, I hit the lights on my way out and made my way back to my room. Dove was still out like a light, so I slid in behind her and pulled her close. For the first time in a long time, I fell asleep within seconds of my head hitting the pillow.

"No ma'am I'm not." I heard Dove say. Reaching over

to the side she slept on. I felt around, but I didn't feel her. I opened my eyes looking around for her. Finally, my eyes landed on her sitting in the window seat, looking over at me. She smiled at me when our eyes connected. "Yes, ma'am, I have three more months then I'll be walking the stage." I pushed myself up and rubbed my face trying to wake up; since my alarm hadn't gone off, I knew it wasn't too late in the day yet. I got out the bed, giving her some privacy to deal with her phone call as I handled my business in the bathroom. After I covered my hygiene and pissing, I hopped in the shower.

Thirty minutes later, I stepped out of the bathroom with a towel wrapped around my waist, refreshed, and ready to start my day. I smiled when I noticed Dove had pulled the sheets off the bed and replaced them with new ones. I was a simple nigga; I wore what I thought was comfortable and didn't care about the tag. I know nigga's that got more LV, Gucci, True Religion, and Prada in the closet, but they don't own shit else. I invested my money instead; I owned a few properties, including my house and my grandmother's, and each car that we drove.

"Hey, I left your food in the microwave; I have a ten o'clock class I need to get to." Dove said as she stepped into the room. I looked her over, from head to toe, her black fitted top, blue jeans, and black and white Air Jordan 1 Retro High OG's looked good on her.

"What other classes you got today?" I questioned as I dropped my towel to pull on my boxer briefs. I laughed a little when her eyes followed the towel, and she licked her lips as she watched my dick. "Man, Dove, answer the question."

"You already know my schedule don't front." She replied, she sucked her teeth and crossed her arms over her chest, pretending to have an attitude.

"Answer the question." I said as I reached for her to pull her closer to me. She came willingly to me and wrapped her arms around my neck. "Drop that little fake ass attitude." I smacked her ass before cupping it in my hands.

"Just the one, then I'm going to run some errands, stop by my house and check in with my little sister Sage and my nephew." Dove responded as she gently ran her fingers over the back of my neck, no lie that shit felt so good. But not good enough that I didn't peep her mention she was going by her spot too.

"Nah, man, wait till later to go by your old spot." I said shaking my head. I let her go and took a step back so she could see how serious I was.

"I just have to make sure I didn't leave any food in the fridge that could spoil. I will be in and out." She responded, she turned around and headed for the door with an extra little umph in her step as she swayed out the room.

"I don't care about all that. Call me when you get back here, and I'll drive you myself." I shouted as I put on my shirt. The door closing was the only response I got from her. "Fucking girl gonna make me kill someone over her ass before she realizes how serious I am." I mumbled to myself as I finished getting dressed.

Thirty minutes after Dove left, I'd eaten the food she had put up for me and was heading down the street. It wasn't much traffic as I hit I-70 going west to get into the city so I could meet up with Benny and the boys so we could start our day.

Dove

"GIRL STOP LISTENING TO LILY, I am not about to be wifed up." I said to Sage as I sat a plate of chicken nuggets and mashed potatoes down in front of him. He smiled up at me before grabbing a nugget and taking a bite of it. I gently pinched his cheek before walking away from him. Since my class was canceled, I finished with my errands sooner than I thought I was, so I grabbed something to eat for myself, my nephew, and sister and planned to spend more time over here than I originally planned. But I knew Sage didn't care, and I hadn't seen my nephew Juke in a while.

"Hey, I'm just asking you what was going on. Lily said yall was looking real cozy together the other night is all." Sage said with a laugh as she used the mirror in front of her to part her hair. Sage and I could pass as twins; if we weren't five years apart, I would believe it myself. The only major difference between the two of us was Sage was about three skin tones darker than I was. "Yall just over there playing house for the last month and ain't said a word to nobody."

"Aint nobody playing house!" I said with a shake of my head. Even though what she said was true, for the last month, CJ and I had been in our little world. We fell into such a smooth and easy routine that the time flew by. I hadn't returned to my house since that night, and CJ had mentioned a few days ago about me just letting it go, but after I explained to him that it was my mama's house and I couldn't, he said he understood. I was thinking about renting it out and pulling in a little extra money, I hadn't mentioned it to him, but I planned to later.

"What you call it then?" Sage said she watched me through the mirror that she was using, and when I didn't answer her right away, she started laughing. "I mean yall cute or whatever and I'm not hating at all, but you gotta be careful with any nigga in the streets. Their lifestyle is dangerous."

"Did Lily tell you about her and Benny?" I questioned as I stood behind her; I took the comb from her hand and fixed her part. I intentionally ignored her comment about CJ being dangerous. Unlike dudes, I'd dated in the past the only thing I worried that CJ could damage was my heart. Physically I knew he wouldn't hurt me.

"Girl yes, Lily tries to front like she not feeling Benny like that, but I know she is. I know I always hear about the crew he runs with; it's all Bleus talks about. He respects them niggas, and you know how Bleus is." Sage said with an eye roll, Bleus was her best friend and if you ask me, they were in love with each other even though they denied it. They were always together; he was even listed on her sons' birth certificate even though he wasn't his biological father. Bleus always said it didn't matter that he didn't come from his nuts, he was his seed, and if his bitch ass daddy wanted to handle it like men, they could.

"I like them together. He respects her and if Kane pops back up for any reason then he gonna wish that he didn't." I said in between making funny faces at my nephew, who sat in his highchair. He was such a cute baby, with chubby cheeks, big round bright green eyes, long curly red hair with sprinkles of freckles running across his face.

"She just doesn't want to try nothing with him cause of what Kane ole' weak ass put her through." Sage said; she sucked her teeth in agitation and rolled her eyes. Kane was Lily's on again off again boyfriend who didn't know how good he had it with her. They started dating around the same time Tika and I did. At first, their relationship seemed like it was going well. Then Lily would start coming over with bruises, black eyes, and a time or two a broken bone. No matter how many times we tried to tell her that he wasn't shit and would keep hitting her, she kept going back. Then she found out she was two months pregnant, she finally stopped going back, and everything was okay. She was getting some shine on her name because of her ability to do nails, had her spot, and was just genuinely happy. When Lily was around seven months pregnant, Kane popped back up, claiming he was different and ready to do right by her, and being the forgiving person; she is, Lily let him back in. They were good for about a month then I got a call from the hospital saying that Lily had been brought in. The hardest thing I've ever had to do was sit next to my beaten and battered sister as she laid on a hospital bed and had her stillborn daughter cut out of her. Kane had beaten her so bad that not only had she lost her daughter but a portion of her lungs, broken leg, arm, and finger, and some hearing in her left ear. She spent the better part of two years in physical therapy, relearning how to write, walk, and take care of herself. And is still in therapy today dealing with the guilt of losing her child, depression, and some PTSD from everything she'd been through.

"I saw them together, and according to CJ, Benny plans to let it be known that he wants to be with her." I said as I straightened her hair with the flat iron; she wiped her head around to face me at the mention of CJ's name. "I'm going to call Tatum and see what she says about it." I said slowly as I tried to figure out her sudden reaction. I raised my eyebrow in question when she didn't say anything. Instead, she sat there, facing me with a goofy smile on her face.

"CJ? Sort of tall, bulky build, thick ass beard, always wears a dope ass fitted and custom shoes?" She questioned; my only response was a single head nod in confirmation. "Why Lily ass didn't tell me? We talk damn near daily, and she never mentioned who you were with. She would just say you were okay and that hubby was taking care of everything."

"Sage, I've mentioned his name before." I said dismissively. Although we didn't talk as much as she and Lily did, we did talk at least three times a week.

"No, the hell you didn't! I would've remembered cause that nigga ain't nobody to play about, like at all big sis. You telling me you messing with the second in command of TCB and ain't tell me?" Sage said she was more so talking to herself than she was talking to me. "I should've known cause he runs with Benny and if you talking about Benny, then it ain't no way you ain't at least run into CJ at least once."

"What the hell are you talking about, Sage?" I questioned, I turned Sage around by her shoulders so I could finish the last part of her hair. Silently I wrecked my brain trying to figure out how I missed it, the way he moved, how people stopped whatever they were doing whenever he was around. He wasn't just a regular hood nigga; he didn't just have the pull to be able to walk freely. This man lived and breathed danger. He said certain things now made sense, like in class, he told me I wasn't ready to mess with a nigga like him, or when we were talking, and he kept mentioning he was prepared to step down. I always thought he was just ready to step out of the game and live a regular life.

"Dove, are you trying to tell me that you didn't know who CJ was? Like, how didn't you know?" She questioned; I could tell she was dumbfounded by my response because I was beyond confused as to what she was talking about. "How did you meet him cause yall don't run in the same crowd."

"Class, we have a few of the same classes." I replied as I finished the last piece of her hair. I stepped back and stared at her for a few seconds to make sure she wasn't joking. Still, my heart was racing like I'd just ran a marathon. Before she could tell me, what was going on, my phone rang; I picked it up from the coffee table and rolled my eyes at Red's name flashed across my screen. I let it go to voice mail only to have her call me over and over before I finally picked up the phone.

"Hello?" I answered, I knew she could tell I had an attitude, but I didn't care. I hadn't heard from her since she hung up on me at her mama's BBQ. I wasn't a person who thought you should check in with your friend every second of the day, but I'm sure she heard about what happened by now. And if she was my friend, she should've at least text me to see if I was okay. But I hadn't heard from Red in a month, and her distance told me so much about her that I never saw before.

"Girl, what you doing?" Red asked; I could hear a bunch of noise in her background, but I wasn't sure if it was the tv or actual people. With Red, you never could tell unless she wanted you to, there were times she would record background noise and play it while talking to the person, so they thought she was elsewhere.

"What do you want, Red?" I questioned; I sat the flat iron down and stepped back to check Sage's hair.

"What's with the attitude?" Red said as she sucked her

teeth. "You at home, I was going to slide through and see if you wanted to hang for a little."

"No, I'm with Sage." I said. I intentionally didn't give her my exact location because just Lily Sage couldn't stand Red either, and I refused to bring drama to my sister's home. Not only would I feel bad for it because of my nephew, but my sister stayed out of the drama.

"You ready for the tea?" Red questioned; she didn't give me a chance to respond before she continued talking. "Girl Tika out here trippen, talking about he going after TCB, and he doesn't care if the street declared CJ off limits cause of how his people are. He has already been robbing his dope boys and even plans to hit a couple of his trap houses tonight. Word on the street is he owns that club we were at not too long ago, so he said he shooting that bitch up too." She let out a loud laugh, I could hear her clapping her hands too like someone had just told her the funniest joke in the world, and she couldn't stop laughing.

"Red, let me call you right back, girl. Sage needs me for something." I said. I tried like hell to keep the panic out of my voice. She was talking too much, which meant she was drunk already this early in the day, but that shit worked in my favor this time because I needed to warn CJ.

"Alright then girl, call me later." Red responded; I hung up the phone and looked up at Sage. This shit with Tika was getting out of hand.

"Girl, that shit is crazy; you are dating a nigga that your ex considers the opp. And has for a long ass time." Sage responded as she got up from her chair and started to clean up; her son had fallen asleep in his highchair, one nugget still in his hand. I didn't even try to respond to her. Instead, I quickly pulled up my text message thread with CJ. My mind was racing with a million thoughts; how didn't I know? Yeah,

I stayed to myself and just lived my life, but I should've known. It explained why Tika reacted the way he did when he saw him; he'd been planning for months, even when we were together, on how to take over the TCB territory. He'd been doing low hits on his boys and jacking his suppliers lately, and the only reason I knew that was because Red ran her mouth about his business all the time. "This shit messy."

Me: Where you at?

CJ: With Benny, making a few runs on the east side. What's up?

Me: We need to talk. Can you meet me at my house? I know you said don't go there without you but it's closer than me coming to your house.

CJ: Where you at now? I can just come to you.

Me: I'm with Sage, her house is on the west side. It would be quicker if I just met you at my house.

CJ: Meet you there in twenty.

Me: Be careful

CJ: You too, baby

I let out a sigh of relief as I put my phone back in my pocket. Without realizing it, I started to pace, this shit was too much, and I needed to talk to CJ before I lost my nerve. I knew enough about Tika's operation to know that he was slimy as hell and more than likely, and if Red was running her mouth freely, then he'd already called his boys in and had his plan ready for action.

"Sage, I'm about to head out; I will call you later." I threw over my shoulder as I headed towards the door. I picked up my purse and was out the door before she could say anything.

The normal twenty-minute ride to my place took about ten. I sped the entire way there, ran a few lights, and hit a few corners too hard, but it didn't matter. The only thing I wanted to do was see CJ and make sure he knew about Tika's stupid ass plan. The entire ride, I kept going over everything Red and Sage told me. CJ was second in command of TCB; they made a name for themselves a few years ago as being hitters, then they started branching out and now had their hands in everything. People respected them because they lived by the OG's rules and left families out of it; if they had a problem with you, they came to you. They weren't shooting up the neighborhoods because of beef. If they saw you out with your kid, they let you go with a warning that the next time they were coming for you, you better be alone cause that one pass is all you got. They took care of the neighborhood kids and old folks. Did holiday drives and policed our neighborhoods better than the police did. Red had mentioned over the last year or so that Tika wanted a bigger piece of the pie and started getting antsy. When he started pulling small jobs against the TCB, everybody in the hood was talking cause they knew it was going to be a war eventually once they found out who was behind it.

I pulled into my driveway; the neighborhood kids were out playing a basketball game that was going on in the middle of the block. Tiny and her little friends looked like grown women as they sat on the curb, drinking pop and eating ice cream as they watched the boys' play. I got out of the car and looked around before going to sit on my porch. I dropped my head into my hands and waited for CJ; I didn't even see the point of going in.

"Ms. Dove, where you been at? Word around the neighborhood is that TCB snatched you up a few weeks ago at a BBQ." Tiny questioned; I raised my head to watch her as she walked through my grass to get to my porch. Her little clique of friends right behind her, all snickering at her comment. Tiny was the only kid on the block that I messed with; she reminded me of my oldest sister Falcon. Book smart but carried her street smarts like it was a badge of honor, and for hood kids, it was. I just hoped the hood didn't get ahold of her like it did Falcon and never let her go.

"I didn't get snatched up Tiny." I said, leaning back in my seat. I looked around briefly before bringing my attention back to Tiny.

"Well, that crazy dude been by your house every day. My mama said he desperate and weak for chasing behind a female that doesn't want him." Tiny said with a shrug of her shoulders. The fact that Tika had been by my spot every day wasn't something to ignore. That would be something else I'd let CJ know, especially since I've been staying with CJ for about a month. He was popping up at my house but wasn't calling or texting me.

"Anybody else been coming by?" I asked; something wasn't sitting right with everything going on. Tika wasn't a quiet type of person unless he was up to something.

"Just him and your friend with the mix-matched name and hair color." Tiny said with a shrug. "My mama said she ain't no real friend to you, but you ain't hear that from me, Ms. Dove."

As if she knew we were talking about her Red's all-black Tahoe came around the corner. I stood from the chair and watched as she eased down the street, the boys got out her way, but she still kept the slow pace. Something about how slow she was moving didn't sit right with me, as I started to reach for Tiny the back window rolled down and two guns were aimed right at us.

Bam! Bam! Bam! Bam! Bam! Bam!

I pushed Tiny down and dropped to the ground, covering my head. It felt like forever before the gunshots stopped. I didn't move immediately because I knew they could just be reloading, or someone could start shooting back and I didn't want to get hit in the crossfire. Because of blood rushing to my ears and the loud beating of my heart beating when I dropped down, I didn't hear the car doors open or the footsteps coming towards me until it was too late, and Tika stood over me smiling.

"Get your stupid ass up!" Tika yelled as he snatched me up by my shirt; he pulled me to my feet so fast that I stumbled a little before I caught my balance. "I been looking for your ass for a month!" He was so mad that spit was flying from his mouth each time he said something. "I was coming over here damn near every day, beating at your door like I'm a simple ass nigga. All I wanted to do was talk! Tell you that I was ready, I been trying to prove to you how serious I was! I stopped fucking with other bitches, even had them abort my seed cause I saw how bad it hurt you last time! Look at what I had to do to get your attention!" He jerked me away from him so that I could see the neighborhood; my eyes bounced from the bodies lying on the ground before I brought my focus back on him.

"I didn't make you do this, Tika; you chose to." I mumbled, which only made him madder; he let go of my shirt's collar and grabbed me by the throat. "Let me go Tika." I grabbed his wrist with one hand and tried to pry his fingers from around my throat with the other.

"Nah this shit is your fault. These people gotta bury their family cause you'd rather be a stupid thot bitch and run to the opp like I'm some type of joke." He pulled me closer to his face; this time, our faces were less than an inch apart. "Didn't I tell you I'd kill yo stupid ass before I let somebody else, have you?! You thought I was playing? Do you think I give a shit about that nigga CJ or TCB? I don't! let me let you in on a little secret." Tika moved his mouth to my ear and spoke so lowly that only he and I knew what he said. "I got about thirty niggas now running him down on the highway, he ain't gonna make it in time to save yo stupid ass and when I leave here I'm on my way to his grandmama house he got in the burbs to put a bullet in her ass."

"I'd rather be with the opp than a weak ass nigga like you." I said as I pulled back from Tika. He had a good grip on me, so I didn't move too far away from him. With a smirk on his face, he backhanded me across the face, making me fall to my knees. I squeezed my eyes closed and shook my head to stop the ringing in my ears. Tika grabbed me by the collar again, opened my eyes in time to see his fist coming towards my face. He hit me in my eye so hard I'm pretty sure he broke my eye socket, and he didn't stop until I was on all fours, and then he kicked me in the stomach. My entire body hurt from his hits and kicks, but I didn't cry out for help. Honestly, I wasn't sure if I could because of the pain I felt.

"Tika!" I heard Red scream. I forced my swollen eyes open to see her grab Tika by his arm and pull him away from me. I laid there, trying to catch my breath, hoping that someone would help me.

"Get in the car baby!" Tika yelled at Red before turning his attention back to me. If this situation wasn't so fucked up, I would've laughed. It turns out Lily and Auntie were right all along; Tika and Red were messing around. Without moving my head, I watched Red run to the car; not once did she try and check on me; her full attention was on Tika and doing what he said. "You never was worth the trouble. I was just with you cause your bitch ass daddy wanted me to look after you." Tika said as he crouched down to talk to me as I laid there on my stomach in pain. "I told that nigga he should've just put a bullet in yall asses and went about his life, but he wanted to let yall live." He used his gun to push my braids out my face so I could see him. "Don't worry about it though, I'll do what that nigga didn't have the courage to do." I watched as he stood up and cocked his gun, but my attention wasn't on him. Instead, my focus went in between his feet to Tiny's watery eyes as she laid across from me, gasping for air. She reached her hand out to me, trying to get a connection to someone as she fought to stay alive. My heart broke for her family, she's only twelve, she has her entire life in front of her, but she was losing a battle in a war. She wasn't even apart of it. I reached to Tiny, I let out a small sigh of relief when our hands met, and she squeezed my hand. Tika stood above me, still going on and on in a rant while I kept my eyes connected to Tiny. I was going to die I rather look at someone I know loved me instead of a person who I knew from his actions alone had never cared.

*Bam!

I heard, then felt the bullet enter into my back. The last thing to cross my mind was my family. Sage, Falcon, Lily, Bleu, Tatum, Auntie, Benny, Ms. Clever, Constance, my mama, and CJ's face all flashed before my eyes before everything went black.

7

Cj

"Bro, little Dove got you acting like a changed man." Benny said as we cruised down I-70 headed towards the city. We had Focus bumping through the speakers and our blunts were rolled so perfectly that we didn't want to smoke them in the car, instead, we sat them to the side for our at home smoke session with our ladies.

"Same way Lily got your ass out the streets and at home?" I questioned with a laugh; I turned down the music just a little so that we weren't yelling over it, trying to talk to each other.

"Man get the fuck outta here with that shit!" Benny said, he waved off my comment but didn't deny it. I was happy for my guy, though; Lily was good for him. She wasn't after his money, nor did she give a damn about what the bitches in the street were saying cause she knew it was her he was with every night.

"You ain't gotta front out and be boosie cause you know it's true." I said as I adjusted my fitted over my eyes to block the sun out. "Every time I check in on yo ass you with her, just came from seeing her, or on your way to see her before doing a run."

"We talking about you and Dove nigga, not me and Lily." He said as he got off the highway, he made a left on Jackson. The normal panhandler that sat out there waved at us as we passed him. Most people didn't pay that nigga any mind, and I appreciated it since he was on my payroll and let me know who came and went down the highway. I made a mental note to drop him a few stacks on the way back later. "You pretty much playing house and shit at this point."

"Nigga that's my baby," I said as I pulled the sun visor down and checked my face in the mirror. I tilted my head side to side, checking to make sure my beard was still moisturized and didn't look nappy. I licked my lips and shook my head at the thought of Dove riding my face last night; after she was finished, she told me the only reason my beard had gotten so thick since we started fucking was cause pussy juice was good for beards. I laughed so hard at her ass that I had to pee, but I couldn't front out on her, my shit had thickened up a lot, and I kept my face in her pussy almost daily. "I told you when I saw her that day on campus that I was going to make her mine."

"Nigga you did." Benny said with a head nod as we came to a stoplight. I looked over at Central High. It was my old stomping grounds while in high school. Benny and I stayed in the principal's office or chilling at the pool. We had damn near straight A's, so they didn't say too much to us, plus the shady ass Superintendent at the time was on my Uncle payroll. So, if I was sent to this office all he would do was send me on my way. "Aye, how we end up fucking with sisters though?"

"Shit nigga we family so it's only right our women are too." I said with a shrug as he pulled off.

Benny didn't even look over at the screen to see who was calling him when his phone rang. It was a handful of people who had the number, so he knew it was personal and never work.

"Yeah mama what's up?" Benny said after his blue tooth connected his phone call.

"Benny!" Lily yelled into the phone. "Benny, where are you? Is CJ with you?"

"Yo Lily, calm down, baby!" Benny said, turning the corner; I raised the speaker's volume so he could hear her better. "What's going on? Why you trippen?"

"Benny, somebody shot up Dove's block!" Lily yelled into the phone; I could hear keys jingling and a crying baby in the background. I pulled my phone out of my pocket, I swiped away all the missed calls and unanswered text messages and pulled up Dove's number.

"Lily, baby, are you sure?" Benny questioned; he didn't even look over at me as he pulled over a few blocks from Dove's spot. Our detour could cost us a few seconds, but if something about this shit didn't sit right with me. I kept redialing Dove's number, but she wasn't picking up and that shit was pissing me off even more. She knew to answer my phone calls when I called and if she couldn't talk for whatever reason to text me right back.

"Yes! I'm with Sage now and we are headed that way!" Lily yelled into the phone.

"Yo is this Benny?" A man's voice said came through the phone before Benny could get a word out to calm Lily down.

"Nigga, who the fuck is this, and why you got my woman's phone?!" Benny yelled into the phone as he hit another corner. People saw us coming and moved out our way, I didn't doubt even a little bit that he'd run their asses over and not give to fucks about it right now.

90

"Yo, my name Bleus. I'm her sister Sage's best friend."
Bleu's responded, he didn't sound offended or upset at
Benny's questioning him. "I got a few of my boys on the
way to the area, as back up. I don't know what yall walking
into, and I know yall got yall boys, but I'm sending some
more friendly faces into the mix. I got Lily and Sage with
me." Bleus said calmly.

"Yeah, I appreciate that man." Benny said with a head
nod. "Keep Lily with you until I hit you back up." Benny
didn't fuck with a lot of people, and if he did consider you
someone he fucked with, then he would go wild making
sure you were safe. If Bleus could keep Lily out the streets
for even a short time while we checked things out, then he
was helping keep my nigga sane for a little bit.

"Fuck all that shit! That's my sister! She could be hurt!
We can't get her or nobody else on the block to pick up the
phone; I'm going." Lily yelled in the background. "I'm
calling Falcon, I bet nigga's start talking when she
shows up."

"Shit, don't call that girl Lily!" Bleus yelled at her. "Lily,
I will take you over there once we get an all-clear. The last
thing we fucking need is her trigger happy ass coming in
there and shooting every muthafucka who looks at her like
she crazy."

"Nah don't take your ass over there! CJ and I ain't too
far from there." Benny said as he cut the car off and
hopped out. He didn't wait for Lily to respond before he
hung up the phone and sprinted towards the back of the
house. We had a few houses in the area that nobody knew
about that we stashed a few cars at; just in case we needed
to switch up, I put in the code for the garage, and thank-
fully it didn't take long for the door to open completely. I
ran inside and hoped in; I kept the key inside the car, so all
I had to do was press the start button and pulled out with

Benny behind me in his truck. Now I know it doesn't seem like the smartest thing to do is waste time by switching cars, but I said something wasn't sitting right with me about all this. We needed to come through in something they hadn't seen just in case they had a few people waiting to finish the job. The hood was fucked up like that; folks didn't care if you were mourning the loss of someone or celebrating a birth. When they were ready to shoot, then the bullets were coming, no matter the situation.

We pulled up to Dove's block a few minutes later; police, ambulance, and news reporters were everywhere. I parked my truck in the middle of the street and hopped out. I truly only gave a fuck about finding Dove and making sure she was okay. Looking around I saw people standing on their porches watching as other people screamed and hollered over their loved one's bodies. I watched as a woman broke down in the middle of the street, a young child limp in her arms that was dead. I dropped my head for a second and said a prayer for them, kids were not to be fucking touched, yet it was obvious a muthafucka didn't give a shit about that no more.

"Aye man you CJ right?" I raised my head slowly and watched as a tall skinny rasta looking nigga made his way towards me. I nodded my head and raised my shirt to show him my nine. "Bleus sent us, I'm Trigga." He nodded towards the group of men standing on the side. I barely looked at them, even though Bleus sent him. I didn't know them or that nigga.

"I'm trying to find my woman, you seen her?" I questioned Trigga. Wasn't any need for pleasantries or getting to know everybody; we were here to find one person and one person only.

"Nah, but I got my boys looking for her; I know Dove from the block. My auntie and cousin live over here."

Trigga said as he looked around. Trigga had to stand close to 6'7, yellow as hell, skinny as hell; he had a long face and droopy eyes with some long ass wild locs that looked like they were only retwisted once every few years; he reminded me of a light skin version of Snoop Dogg.

"You checked on yo people yet?" I asked, even though I didn't care, but I asked out of respect. This shit was a blood bath and if his people were safe and unharmed that meant his focus would be fully on finding Dove.

"Nah, but I got a different set of folks looking for them." Trigga said with a shake of his head. "When we got here, they said the ambulance had already carried off about six people, but we caught this little nigga running his mouth." Trigga waved over at his crew; a short dark nigga I'd seen around the block a few times came forward, pushing a kid forward. "This Dutch, he caught this little nigga flapping his gums talking about his cousin did this shit."

"Who yo cousin little nigga?" I asked him once he was within reaching distance. I watched as he smirked at me before crossing his arms over his chest.

"You know how my people are." He said with a laugh, he just didn't know he was looking around like he was waiting on someone to hype his stupid ass up. This is what I hated about little niggas; a lot of times, they rode the coattails of other people. He bragging about a nigga who ain't out here cause he knows what he did is fucked up, and his life would be ended soon.

"Nigga you think I give a fuck about the police standing around here?" I said; I pulled him closer to me by his collar. "I will put a bullet in your fucking skull and walk away from this bitch like nothing happen. So, if you want yo mama to be like that lady over there clenching yo cold body against her. Screaming in the street, you might want to stop trying to front and let me know who did this shit so I can find my woman and get the fuck out of here."

"Fuck you," He said with a snarl on his face; I pushed him back towards Trigga and shook my head. Stupid ass little nigga. "Bring his stupid ass with us; if he wants to play games, I'll feed his body to the pigs, and his mama will never get closure." At my words, his eyes bucked out their sockets, but I didn't give a fuck. My only concern was finding Dove and getting her the fuck out of here.

"Aye Trigga, I got word on yo people!" A young cat said, running up to Trigga and me.

I stepped back, giving Trigga the space he needed to talk to his young bull, tapping Benny on the arm getting his attention; I nodded my head towards the cop we had on the payroll. We made our way over, still looking around for Dove but giving people the respect, they deserved as they mourned the loved ones they'd lost.

"Aye, Stone, let me holla at you for a second." Benny said when we were close enough to him. Stone nodded his head and excused himself from the person he was talking to. We stood next to a black Tahoe that sat on top of a tow truck. It didn't have any bullet holes in it, which told me this was what the shooter came in but didn't leave in it. "What you know so far?"

"So far, nobody is talking, and the little chatter we have is saying that whoever came here started shooting. Cleared out this entire area before getting out his car and going to that house right there." Stone said, pointing to Dove's house; my heart stopped for a second before starting back up, beating so fast I'm pretty sure it could break out my chest. "We had to rush them to the hospital. It was a woman and a little girl. The shit is bad; they don't know if either of them is going to make it."

"What hospital did they go to?" I questioned, I damn

near growled that shit out, but I didn't care. My woman's house was shot up, meaning she was the intended target. That shit told me that without a doubt it was Tika's weak ass that did it.

"Truman." Stone said. "CJ-" I didn't even wait for him to keep talking. The shit didn't matter; I needed to get my ass down to Truman and quick. I damn near pushed people out the way as I made my way towards my truck, I didn't even need to look back to see that Benny and the boys were right behind me. I jumped into my truck, started it, and pulled off without giving a damn about anyone's safety.

Ten minutes later I was rushing through the ER doors of Truman, I rushed to the nurse's station, beating on the desk to get someone's attention since no one was there.

"Aye! Yo!" I said as I repeatedly hit my palm on the countertop. "Yo!"

Finally, a heavy-set white woman came from the back with a chicken wing in her mouth; immediately, I could tell I was going to have to choke this bitch out because of her raggedy ass attitude. "You don't have to keep yelling; I'm coming." She said with a huff after she sat down in her chair; she threw the wing into the trash, with the same greasy hand she tapped on the computer's keyboard a few times to wake it up.

"I'm looking for my girlfriend; they said she was brought here." I said; I pulled my glasses off my face and rubbed my eyes, trying to control my anger. She rolled her eyes and sucked her teeth before she started typing away.

"What's your girlfriends' name? Why was she brought in?" Nurse, with an attitude, questioned as she popped her gum. I pinched the bridge of my nose and let out a deep breath, saying a silent prayer to the man above for the patience to deal with her.

"Dove Lincoln, she was brought in for gunshot wounds. She was a part of the shooting on Brooklyn." I said, putting my glasses on. I waited as she started typing again. "Ma'am, I'm not trying to be rude, but I'm in a rush and would like to make sure she is okay."

"Look, I'm searching that database right now." She responded, she stopped and looked up at me and waited. "You have two choices; you can wait until I'm done eating my lunch that you rudely interrupted, or you can give me a few seconds while I look up her name and see where she's at."

I didn't say anything, which caused her to nod her head and start looking again. "I need your ID." She said reaching her hand up without looking at me. I pulled my wallet out of my pocket and handed it to her. I knew the routine when it came to visitors and shooting victims. Since it was common for the shooter or someone associated with them to come and see if the person was dead or not, the local hospitals started making copies of the visitor's IDs just in case something happen to them while they were there. A few seconds later, she handed me my ID back and pointed to the sign-in sheet. I scribbled my name down after I put my ID away and continued to wait.

"Have a seat over there." She said, pointing to the far right corner of the waiting room without looking up still. "The doctors will be out shortly to talk to you, just a word to the wise if she makes it. Keep your girl out the middle out of whatever shit you're a part of. They targeted that girl."

Again, I didn't respond, even though I wanted to tell her to mind her fucking business. I made my way to the corner of the room and sat down, dropping my head into my hands; I did the only two things I knew to do. I prayed and waited.

8

Lily

"I don't know, Auntie; we are pulling up now. Benny called and said the cops took Dove to Truman. CJ is already there." I pointed to an open spot towards the front of the parking lot that was close to the door.

"Okay, I'm getting off the highway now; I'll find y'all when I get there." Constance said before hanging up. I threw my phone in my purse that sat between my feet, I let out a deep breath, trying to steady my racing heart as Bleus pulled into the spot and threw the car in park. I didn't wait for him to unlock the door; I pulled the lock up and hopped out of the car, grabbing my purse before closing the door with Sage and Bleus right behind me. The three of us made our way through security and headed towards the nurse's station to try and get an update on Dove.

The minute that Benny called and said that she'd been taken to Truman I knew it was going to be bad. Any and everybody knew you only went to Truman if you were shot, it was a running joke in KC that if you went in there for anything else other than that then you were going to wish you were shot by the time you left. The news of the shooting had already been blasted all over the news and radio, the entire car ride over; I'd been getting calls and texts from people that knew my sister lived on that block, trying to make sure she was okay.

"Excuse me!" I yelled, banging on the empty nurse's desk countertop. I waited for someone to come out the back. This was another reason people hated this hospital, there wasn't ever anyone around to help you, and when they did finally showed up, they always had an attitude like you were wrong for wanting them to do their job. "Excuse me!"

"What is it this time?!" A fat white woman said, coming from a side door I hadn't noticed when I first walked in. "Yall can't just come in here yelling!" I wanted to smack the shit out of her, but I knew that it wouldn't get me anywhere but dragged down to the jail and catch a charge for assault.

"Ma'am, we are looking for our sister; her name is Dove Lincoln." Sage said stepping up to stand next to me, she knew how short my temper was and knew to start before I could open my mouth. The fat bitch had the nerve to look at us like we were crazy before rolling her eyes and sticking out her hand, we all handed her the IDs that we still have in our hands since coming through security. She snatched them from us, typed in a few things, and pointed over our heads.

"Go sit by the boyfriend and wait for the doctors to come out." The stupid bitch didn't even have the decency to hand us back our ID's. Instead, she dropped them on the countertop, got up from her chair, and disappeared back into the door she came out of.

"I swear once we find out what's going on with Dove, I'm waiting for that bitch in the parking garage." I said, turning around; I looked around the room before my eyes landed on CJ, who had his head resting in the palm of his hands. I knew Benny was on his way with the rest of his boys, but to see him sitting there by himself waiting on news about Dove hit me hard. "That's CJ over there." I threw my head in his direction and made my way towards him. He must have felt us watching him because he slowly raised his head out of his hands and watched us; he stood when we were within a few feet of him.

"I haven't heard anything, and the bitch at the nurse's station hasn't done anything but stuff her fat ass mouth with food." CJ said answering our unspoken question.

"Okay." I responded as I took a seat, Bleus and Sage sat next to me and CJ sat across and we waited. "Our auntie is on the way."

He didn't verbally respond, only nodded his head and dropped his face back into his hands. We sat there quiet, each of us lost in our thoughts; it was like we were afraid to say anything because we were waiting on pins and needles for a word about Dove.

"Lily!" I heard. Turning my head, I waved Constance over; standing, I let her pull me into a hug that I knew she desperately needed. She let me go and pulled Sage and Bleu into hugs as well before sitting down next to me. Again, we sat in silence; every so often, CJ's phone would go off with a text; he would respond, then drops his head back down. I watched him at first, I thought he was talking to him, trying to calm himself down some type of way then I realized he was praying. Saying the same prayer over and over, as he bit into a cross he had around his neck.

The entrance door flew up, and in walked the prettiest woman I'd ever seen in my life. I could tell from her hurried footsteps she wasn't trying to make an entrance, but she did without trying. Her hand came to her throat and she gripped onto whatever hung around her necklace.

She searched the room and let out a deep breath when her eyes landed on CJ who still hadn't raised his head yet. She had dark brown skin, the color of a good Louisiana roux for gumbo, a small curvy frame, a small, pointed chin, thick lips, a cute little button nose, and small slanted eyes. Her hair was cut into a cute bob that fit her face perfectly, and her hair so black that it almost looked blue when the light hit her. She wore a pair of dark orange linen pants, with a white sleeveless linen shirt that gathered around her neck, her two-strap open-toed heels were the same color as her pants, she went simple with an iced out watch, a single ring on her right hand and cheetah print purse rested on the crook of her arm. Her eyes searched the room before landing on CJ, and she made her way towards us.

"CJ!" She said, her voice was so smooth that it seemed to wrap around each of us and give us a mother hug we all desperately needed. CJ's mouth stopped moving but he didn't raise from his seat, she gently placed her hand on his back, and that's when it happen. This street nigga that everyone feared, who we knew was a killer and showed no mercy for anyone else in the world, broke, and the tears started flowing. "Have you heard anything?"

"No, ma'am, we're waiting for the doctor to come out." I said speaking up so that CJ could get his tears and emotions under control. The woman continued to rub his shoulders but looked over at us; she gave us a sympathetic smile.

"You must be Dove's sisters and aunt." She said, sitting down next to CJ again. Her hand never left him, and he continued to let the tears fall. "I'm CJ's grandmother."

"Excuse me did you say grandmother?" Sage questioned; I didn't blame her; this woman sitting across from us didn't look any older than 40; there was no way she had damn near a 30-year-old grandson. When she nodded, I didn't say a word, I planned to ask her whatever her secret was when all this was over. "Wow, but yes you are right. We are Dove's sisters. I'm Sage; this is my best friend Bleus, Sage, and our Aunt Constance."

"It's nice to meet you all; I just wish it was under better circumstances." CJ's grandmother said; without looking over at her grandson, she pulled out a tissue from her purse and handed it to him. "Every time I see Dove, she tells me about you all. Once she is out of here and feeling better, we all have to get together."

"That sounds good." Sage said. I appreciated her positive attitude; she was putting good vibes out and not allowing negative thoughts towards Dove and her situation to be around us.

"I'm sorry we didn't catch your name." I said turning my attention from my phone that was constantly going off with a text from Benny, who was on his way. When I told him CJ's grandmother had just shown up, all he responded was, don't let her out my site. Her house had just been shot up and he was out looking for her. This shit was a lot deeper than we realized. This wasn't just some random shooting; people close to CJ were being targeted. I handed my phone to Bleu so he could see the text, he handed me back the phone and pulled his own out. More than likely sending a text to a few of his boys to stand by for further instructions.

"Oh, I'm Clever Jones." Ms. Clever said, finally letting go of her neck and extending her hand for us to shake. We shook her hand and then she sat back in her chair, crossing one leg over the other. Every so often, she'd whisper something in CJ's ear, which cause him to nod his head. Benny showed up shortly after, and we sat around waiting, hoping, and even praying that Dove pulled through.

CJ

"NO ONE SAW ANYTHING, from what I could pull from Stone was that they rolled up on the block in the Tahoe and started blasting from each window and the sunroof." Benny said in between pulls of his blunt; we sat in his living room, the game was on, but neither of us was paying any attention to it. "When they finally stopped blasting, Tika jumped out of the car and ran up on her. They had a few words, he got mad at something she said to him and he hit her a few times." He stopped to allow me to calm down, it took a few seconds, but I nodded my head, letting him know to continue. "Then her friend Red."

"That bitch ain't her friend." I said cutting him off.

"Yeah, that shit true." Benny nodded. "Well, that bitch Red came pulling up and tried to pull him away; they had a few words too. He pushed her back to the car she rolled up in, then he popped Dove a few times and rolled off with Red."

"We got any word on where is he hiding at?" I questioned; I pulled out my phone, checking the time and making sure I hadn't missed any calls from Dove's sisters. It's been a little over a month since the shooting, and it was touch and go for Dove for the first week. She was shot three times in the back and twice in the leg. The ones in her back hit her lungs, kidneys, and liver. She lost a piece of her lung and one of her kidneys, but we were thankful that she survived. The two bullets in her leg went straight through, missing the bone. I thanked the man above daily that Tika wasn't a shooter cause had that been someone else that knew how to aim, they would've killed her.

"A couple of days ago, some chatter started about him hiding out in Oklahoma, but I can't say for sure." Benny said with a shake of his head. "I got a few people out that way that put some feelers out, but until then, I don't know."

"What about that bitch Red?" I questioned, pulling out my favorite Chiefs rolling tray from under the couch. I sat in my lap and started breaking down some weed. In the last month, I've smoked more than I had in my entire life to calm my nerves. Not only did Tika shoot Dove, but he also shot up my grandma's house, he hit my stash house and tried to burn down my club and the few houses I had around the city. I had the police knocking on my door damn near daily, talking about they were investigating my businesses because the fire department said my shit was an inside job.

"From what I been told, Falcon looking for her ass." Benny replied, he dropped his phone on the couch and went back to smoking. "If you want me to try and pull her off I can but we already know how sis gets down so iono even see the reason to at this point."

"True but send word to a few of our people so they can know to keep an eye out anyway." I said with a nod; Falcon was the oldest of the Lincoln sisters and more than likely the craziest. She was a street nigga to the fullest, taking no mercy on any person who crossed paths with her. Unlike her sisters, she stayed in the streets because that's how their mama Rose raised her; when Rose was out doing deals and pushing work, she kept Falcon right next to her. She was prepping her to take over, but Falcon loved the smell of gun powder more. Then when their mother was sent to jail, she pushed harder in the streets. Damn shame too cause the girl was probably one of the smartest people I'd ever met.

"Yeah, let Falcon have it for now." I said.

"How is Grandma doing?" Benny questioned.

"Shit nigga you know how my baby is; she raised hell the entire time I had my boys cleaning out her spot. That was her house for nearly fifteen years, she ain't want to leave that bitch. Talking about she got something for they ass if they come back." I lit my blunt and inhaled deeply; I released the smoke through my nose as I shook my head. "I was dealing with Moose and his loud talking ass, threatening to come out of retirement, bumping his gums talking about I can't take care of her like I'm supposed to. It took everything in me not to pay his punk ass a visit, Dove being in the hospital, and then her stubborn ass. Shit, just stressful." My relationship with Moose was complicated; he was my granny's youngest son who lived on the Kansas side and swore he was the toughest nigga to walk the streets. I hadn't fucked with Moose since it came out, he was the reason my pops was a deadbeat, and my mom was in the streets on that shit. Back in the day, Moose laced their weed with some powder and didn't tell them, shit he ain't tell nobody nothing until I was about twenty years old, and we sat down and smoked together. He offered me some of his weed, and the shit didn't look right, so I asked him what he had on it, and this stupid ass nigga started jaw jacking. Talking about it's the same shit he got my moms and pops hooked on all those years ago. That shit didn't sit right with me, so I asked him to explain, and that's when he told me that he'd laced their weed back in the day because they were complaining that the shit he brought them was weak. My moms got hooked, but by the time my pops realized what was going on, she was too far gone.

I was about five, but I remember them fighting over the bag that Moose had dropped off earlier that day, then my moms ran out of the house. He ran after her of course and his dumb ass didn't even look back to realize I was in the door watching they ass. I stood there for about an hour, just waiting, hoping they'd pop back up because they usually did. But they didn't that time, and it was getting dark, so I went to lay down; I ended up falling asleep on the couch with the door wide open. The neighbor called Moose, who came and got me; he dropped me off with granny and rolled off, didn't ask me what happen or where my folks were. I didn't see my parents for nearly a year and when I did my moms was completely cracked out, and my pops wasn't too far behind her. Eventually, pops got clean, but he said he couldn't take me in, said I looked too much like my mom's, and he couldn't see my face every day and not miss her.

When I was twelve, granny sat me down and told me that my pops were getting married and we were invited to the wedding. I didn't want to go but I couldn't tell Clever Jones no and live to talk about it another day so the day of the wedding we went. I sat next to granny for the entire wedding, and during the reception, he sat down at the table we were at and spoke to her. Weak ass nigga didn't acknowledge me, but his ass couldn't stop bragging about the kid he had with his wife, his boy, his namesake. I sat there laughing, for a few reasons one I knew the look that went across granny face as he sat there gloating about a kid and life that didn't any of us know about; she was about to go off on this nigga, and I was ready for the show. And for two cause I was named after the nigga. How can you have two different kids with the same name? Nigga was walking around with two kids named King Jones Jr, and when granny pointed that exact thing out to him, he looked her straight in the eye and told her he only had one son, and it was the one by his wife.

It took about ten different people to hold granny back as she went crazy on him, calling him every name in the book besides the one she wrote on her birth certificate. His goofy-ass wife came over trying to figure everything out, and granny let her and everyone else in the room knows that he wasn't shit and he would reap what he sowed. She grabbed my hand, and we left, the next day, we started the process to adopt me, and because he was a punk-ass nigga, King signed over his rights without a fight. I didn't have a problem with granny legally adopting me since she'd raised me since I was five. The only thing I asked was to change my name. I refused to be named after that nigga, and she agreed, the only thing she wanted me to do was to think about my name before I wrote anything down; she didn't want me to regret my decision later. I didn't tell her what I chose when she asked; I told her she would have to wait for my adoption day. So, when we stood up in front of the judge, and my family and the judge asked me my name I proudly told him Clever Jones Jr, but he could call me CJ for short.

"Moose ain't shit, and we know that nigga need attention, ignore him." Benny said; he stood, went to the door, and opened it. He handed the delivery person a tip and closed it, walked back to the couch he was sitting on, and dropped down. "If you want, we can pay his ass a visit after we handle this shit."

"If it wouldn't kill my baby, I swear I would." I said as I reached for my food that Benny sat in front of me. I lifted the lid of my oxtails, rice, and peas and inhaled before grabbing a knife and fork out the bag. "That nigga been testing my patience since I can remember."

"Cause jealous, he knows he can't provide grandma with the same lifestyle you do. You bought her that house, the car she drives, pay her bills, and her groceries. She doesn't want for anything; shit, he calls her and asks for money damn near monthly. That nigga knows her little job doesn't pay her like that, she lives the way she does because of you. That shit fucks with his pride. As a man, I couldn't have another man no matter the relationship besides that being her husband taking care of her. Look at my moms and pops, that's the only nigga I let do for her, and I even give him a hard time about that. And my sisters? They know not to bring no nigga around that cant outdo what my pops and I do for them." Benny said in between bites of his food. He was speaking the truth; he didn't let his people want for shit; he made moves happen because he was raised to never let another nigga do what you should have been doing for the people in your life.

When we were younger, his pops did a seventeen-year bid, leaving Benny in charge, and he took his job seriously. He hustled harder than everyone, making a name for himself in the streets as a hard worker, and the older niggas loved a hard-working young buck. But Benny wasn't working for them, he didn't like answering to anybody, so we became partners. We started pulling our niggas in, and we moved our weight for a while. The streets started paying attention even more because we weren't messy with the shit; we kept our crew under control and didn't cause any problems unless there was a need to. Soon everybody knew who we were and what we were about and started calling us Them Clever Boys or TCB for short.

"Jealousy is a bitch trait, not no niggas. He better get his panties out his ass before I said fuck it and just have to dry my baby's tears as they lower that nigga to the ground." I said then took a bite of my food. My ears perked up when I heard the garage door open; I shook my head and wiped my mouth with a napkin before throwing it on the table and getting up. "I swear I'm going to kick her ass, I told her to call me when she was on her way so I could have the door open." I mumbled to myself as I walked through the kitchen and pulled open the door that was connected to the garage.

I watched as Dove backed her truck into the garage, shut it off, and slowly got out. It was crazy how much she turned me on by just doing simple shit, like her stepping out of the truck had me adjusting my dick in my basketball shorts like I was a young nigga who couldn't control his shit. She stood up and let a deep breath out as she leaned against the car with her eyes closed.

"I told you to stop doing that extra shit and just call me when you're pulling up so I can pull your shit into the garage for you." I said, I made my way towards her, licking my lips, I let out my deep breath. She was standing there, looking good as shit in a pair of black biker shorts and orange fitted shirt made out of the same material, a pair of black and orange Nike shocks, and her hair was freshly braided in some shoulder-length butterfly locs thanks to her sister Sage. "You standing there out of breath and hurting cause you not taking into consideration that you was just on a vent laid up in the hospital less than a month ago."

"I know." She said, opening her watery eyes to stare up

at me. I pulled her gently towards me by the bottom of her shirt and kissed her lips before I placed my forehead against hers. She closed her eyes back, but the tears still slid from the corners of her eyes. "I just want to be able to do the things I could before all this happen. I felt good before I left here, better than I have in a while, but then my side started hurting while I was in class. I didn't think too much about it, so I went to Sage's house to check on her and my nephew, and by the time I got there, I was hurting so bad that all I wanted to do was cry."

"So, you ain't call me?" I questioned. Her only reply was a shoulder shrug, and from the way she winced in pain, I knew she was in even more pain than she wanted to admit. "I would've stopped whatever I was doing to come to you." I pulled back a little and lifted her head and waited for her to open her eyes so she could see how serious I was as I spoke. "Didn't I tell you I fuck with you the hard way? You don't even have to tell me you need me, just call, and when I say your name you just say my name. I will be able to know what you need me by the way you do that. Let that pride shit go and let your man know what you need so I can make sure you got it. You understand me?"

"Yeah, I got you." She said. I didn't wait for her to say anything else. I closed the truck door then picked her up; she wrapped her legs around my waist and her arms around my neck, then dropped her face into the side on my neck. Chuckling a little I adjusted her weight in my arms, and I'm not even going to front. I squeezed her ass in both my hands as I made my way inside. "I didn't eat yet." She mumbled, shaking my head at her. I continued in the house, making my way to the bedroom. I sat her in the bed, kneeled in front of her, slid her shoes off her feet, and threw them under the bed. I'd put them away later, right

109

now. My only concern was getting her something to eat and a pain pill so she could relax and hopefully fall asleep. The entire time tears rolled down her face, standing, I wiped them away before helping her get into the bed and covering her up.

"I'll bring you up something to eat and your medicine in a minute." I said before closing the door. When my foot hit the bottom step, I said a silent thank you to Benny; he'd cleaned up our mess and left some food for Dove on the table. I shot my nigga a text letting him know I appreciated his effort and that I'd hit him up later so we could make a few runs. He responded, letting me know that Dove was fam and he had her back just like he had mine. Plus, he ain't want her to yell at him like she did last time when he ordered some tails for him but didn't remember to get her favorite soup. I grabbed water out of the fridge and made my way back upstairs. I pushed the door open a little more forcefully than I planned to, making it slam against the wall, Dove's eye widens in surprise, and I cursed under my breath.

"Sorry about that." I said, she nodded her head in acknowledgment, but I still felt bad, loud noises still get to her at times. "Benny and I were having oxtail's right before you came home, and he ordered you some oxtail soup cause he knows you love it so much." I said, holding up the bowl; the big smile on her face let me know she was happy about the food. I sat down next to her and handed her the bowl and pills. She happily took the water and pills, popping one in her mouth before downing half the water.

I pulled out one of her study notebooks and opened it; I started to question her as she ate. The only thing she told me when she woke up was, she didn't want this to stop her plans. Yeah, she just like the rest of us wanted to take care of Tika but she wanted to get out of the hood and knew that her education was what she needed to be able to do that. So, I paid a few of her professors a visit and explained what was going on. They agreed to email her the assignments and give her some time to recover. With the help of her sisters and me, she caught back up and was on track to graduate on time. If anyone deserved it, it was Dove.

9

Cj

Later that night, I sat with Benny, Bleus, and Trigga in the back of an old house down hidden in the projects on the north side of the city. I took a pull of my blunt as I watched Tika and his punk ass boys' step inside the house; I got a call a little over an hour ago telling me that he'd finally been spotted.

"This nigga thought he could hide out forever." Bleus said as he passed his blunt to Trigga, who shook his head and continued to stare out the window. This shit was personal to him just like it was for me, his little cousin Tiny and her mama had been shot during the drive-by that Tika did. Her mama didn't make it, and Tiny was still fighting for her life in the hospital. It tore that man up on a daily to watch his kinfolk fight for her life, and since he was the only family she had left, he was there daily to check on her.

"He thinks he invincible cause he sprayed a block full of women, kids, and old folks like that shit ain't a bitch move." Trigga said as he pulled his locs into a ponytail. Since the shooting, I'd been working with Bleus and Trigga to find where Tika was, and in the process, we got to know them. They were the type of niggas I fucked with; they understood the old school rules and respected them.

"Nigga don't know that the whole hood got a death wish for his ass now." Bleus said as he opened his door and got out.

We followed right behind him and got out of the truck, each of us cocking our shit as we made our way towards the house. I didn't doubt in my mind that they weren't prepared for us running up on them, but I couldn't be too cocky and got caught off guard. I had plans to go back to my woman with this nigga blood on me as proof that I'd take over the entire world for her if need be.

It was like something changed in us as we made our way towards the house. With each step we took, our blood started to pump harder. Hyping us up for this shit, we weren't even trying to cover our tracks or be quiet; we wanted them to see our faces before killing them. Benny made it to the side of the house first and peeped through the open kitchen window.

"I can see just them three niggas from earlier, they playing the game it looks like." He said to us there was no reason to whisper because they were so loud on the inside of the house there was no way they would've heard us.

"Any sign of Tika?" I questioned.

"Nah, but we know he is there. It's a door closed right off the kitchen, it's either a bedroom or bathroom." Benny turned around to face us. "I say we kick that bitch in and just drop they bodies."

"Works for me." Trigga said; without another word, he turned around and headed to the front of the house. We surrounded the door, Trigga and I in the middle with Benny and Bleu on the outside. I nodded at Trigga; this nigga cocked his foot up and kicked the door in, using all the anger he had built up as his strength. Just like we thought they had gotten cocky, they were caught by surprise as we rushed into the house.

"Get the fuck down!" I yelled, stepped into the living room; these punks ass niggas looked like a bunch of deer caught in headlights. Their eyes were bugged out, stuck staring at us, with the game controllers in their hands. "You heard what I said!" I yelled at the closet nigga to me, he didn't get a chance to move before I hit him in the head with my gun, and he fell to the ground groaning in pain.

"Where Tika at?" Trigga asks, he had his gun pointed against Tika's boy temple, it was the same one who pulled him away the day at the BBQ. He looked over at me and shook his head while cussing under his breath. "Did you hear what the fuck I said?"

"Nigga he ain't here!" His boy said nigga had to think we were stupid because we just saw him walk into the house a few minutes later. There was no way he wasn't there, and all the noise we were making told me he had to know we were here and was hiding. Bleus stepped around us and went to the door that Benny mentioned earlier; I let out a small laugh when I noticed the light was now off.

"If he ain't here then why that light off that was on just a few seconds ago?" Trigga question, I could see he was struggling to control his anger. He trapped the gun against his forehead as he paced back and forth in front of the door that he'd just kicked in. "Yall about to lose yall life over a nigga hiding in the room like a bitch and yall out here."

"Aye, Benny man, do me a favor and check out the bathroom, and if that nigga in here, drag his bitch out ass by his feet." I said to Benny, he smirked a little and switched places with Bleus. I turned my attention back to his boys; they were all young niggas, maybe twenty-five at the most. "Yall niggas picked the wrong fool to follow." I listened as Benny kicked in the room door, it turns out it was a bathroom. Benny let out a loud laugh.

"Aye, this nigga hiding in the laundry basket." Benny yelled to us. I shook my head and let out a small laugh. This nigga talked the most shit and he was hiding in a fucking laundry basket like a bitch. "Get the fuck out the basket nigga." I could hear them tussle around a little before the door swung open. "I don't even see how yo tall lanky ass fit in that basket."

Shortly after Tika came stumbling into the living room, nigga looked like he was ready to piss on himself. Bleu pushed his boys to their knees, while Benny pushed Tika on his. They were facing each other, the only one not crying or sniffling like a little punk had his head facing down. I tapped Benny on the shoulder and nodded to the one with his head down. Benny stepped around Tika and stood in front of the one I pointed out.

"You the only nigga not sitting here cry and begging for your life." Benny said to him. "Raise your head, little nigga, and look at me when I'm speaking."

Ole boy took a second or two but slowly, he raised his head; I shook my head, Benny stepped back with an amused look on his face, Bleu chuckled as he sat back in his seat, and Trigga stopped pacing and stood there dumbfounded. The toughest nigga on his squad was a female. I checked shorty out a little better as I pulled my blunt from behind my ear and lit it. She was yellow, with a round face, thick lips, a small ass nose that had freckles running across her face, and some bright green ass eyes that were getting dark cause she was mad as hell. I couldn't tell what her hair looks like cause. It was hidden under a black skully; she wore a pair of black joggers and a baggy t-shirt. Her arms and hands were tatted up with some kind of animal design, and If I were paying attention earlier, I would've realized that she was a female by her nails being done.

"You telling me the only one in here not scared is a fucking female?" Bleus questioned. "She ain't dropped one fucking tear while you niggas ballin like newborn fucking babies! That shit alone lets me know that yall weak as hell!"

"Nigga don't you know you don't involve females in the line of fire when you know you got a fucking ticket on your head?" Trigga damn near roared as he pushed past us and yanked up Tika. He shook him like a rag doll before he pulled back and hit him right in the eye. "That's a fucking female nigga! You running around here like the biggest nigga in hood but you over here with snot running out yo fucking nose like you Roscoe from Martin!"

Trigga continued beating the shit out of Tika, and I stood there watching. This is what he needed; it was the only way he would find some peace for losing his aunt and possibly losing his cousin. I took a seat next to Bleus on the couch while Benny put a bullet in each of his boy's heads. The female continued to sit there on her knee's her eyes completely on Trigga beating the shit out of Tika. She looked pissed off, her jaw was clenched, and with every blow that landed on Tika, her hands would ball into a fist.

"You fighting a nigga that can't fight back." She mumbled, I barely heard her, so I know that everybody else had a hard time but even though Trigga's attention was focused on beating Tika's ass he stopped in mid-swing and gave her his full attention.

"What you say?" Trigga questioned her, he let Tika's shirt go and he dropped to the ground with a loud thud. Trigga stepped over Tika's body and stood right in front of her, he dropped down to be eye level with her, and with bloody hands, he turned her face towards him. "What did you say?"

"You fighting a nigga that can't fight back." She repeated herself, her dark green eyes damn near blazed with hatred as she looked at Trigga. "You already put a bullet in his boys, do the same to us, and gone about your life."

"Nah, baby, you don't run shit here; I do. That nigga shot up a block full of innocent people because he can't let go of a woman who doesn't want him." Trigga let get of her face and pointed to Tika who was trying and failing to roll over to his side. "I had to put my auntie in the ground, and her daughter ain't too far behind her. You riding for a nigga that doesn't give a shit about the street code. So that nigga gonna suffer a little before a bullet in his ass."

"Don't give me that shit, none of you niggas are innocent yall shit just ain't caught up with yall." She pulled her face from Trigga's hand. "You think that nigga wrong because he put a bullet in a few folks? Don't yall push weight? Sell guns? And If I remember right Trigga before you came up here from Miami yo people stay stealing girls off the street and selling them. So, nah nigga don't give me that innocent shit you got blood on your hands just like he does."

"What my kin doing don't got shit to do with me. Them niggas know where I stand with that shit that's why I roll with Bleus." Trigga said, standing. I looked over at Bleus, who nodded his head at Trigga's statement. The shit his people were into didn't sit right with me but if he let his people know that and distanced himself then I couldn't be mad at him. "And since you know so much about us baby girl what's your name?"

"Don't tell him shit!" Tika said with a groan; he finally rolled over and was trying to push himself up. Trigga turned around and kicked him in the stomach, which made him fall. Lights flashed two times before we heard car doors slam outside.

"Aye, they outside." Bleus said, he took a look at Tika laying on the floor then shorty who had returned her focus on him. "It's time to roll." Three of Bleu's boys and a few of mine stood outside the house talking; I took a pull of my blunt before making my way out the house.

"Drag that nigga to the van then sweep through it, every hidden space this nigga think he got, find it. Box up his shit and donate it to the local shelters if it looks like someone else could use it. After that, burn this bitch down, so the hood knows this nigga taken care of." I said to my runner; each of them nodded their heads and stepped inside the house.

I stepped over to my boy Mickey, nigga was a beast with numbers but hated being couped up in an office all day but did so cause he didn't want to hear his mama and grandmama mouth about not using his degree. Against his family's wishes, he worked for me, making sure my money always looked legit, he usually never got his hands dirty. But when word got back that Tika had set this shit out cause of Dove, Mickey traded his suit and tie for a nine and skully. "You got shit from here?" I question him as we slapped hands and pulled each other in for a quick hug.

"Yeah, man." He said with a laugh as he let me go. He wiped his hands down his face and shook his head. "It took everything in me to get control of her crazy ass, yall niggas owe me." He was dressed in a pair of fatigue colored joggers, a black shirt, and a pair of black Tims. His locks were loose, but he wore a black skully on his head.

"Big sis was ready to declare war on the whole city?" I questioned as I nodded my head in the direction of the car, inside the oldest Lincoln sat in the front seat. Her dark grey eyes stayed focused on the door as my boys dragged Tika out.

"That's a fucking understatement if I ever heard one. She barraged into my office in her favorite outfit, talking about she just wanted to come see me to tell me she loved me before she went out." Mickey said out a humorless laugh. "Even brought my favorite meal with her."

"You knew the shit was a setup then, huh?" I laughed as I pulled another blunt out and leaned against the car we came in. Mickey pulled out his blunt as he dropped his head, his dreads covered his face.

"Nigga I know my woman well enough to know that she doesn't do shit like that unless she up to something." Mickey said with a laugh, we both turned our attention to the sound of the truck door opened and closing. "Last time she put a bullet in my secretary's car because she said she looked at me too hard one day. Had the woman so fucking scared she quit the next day and moved to South Carolina, and all Falcon did was shrug her shoulders and say she wasn't even trying to hit her, it was just a warning shot."

"Was yall even together then?" I questioned with a laugh. Each of the Lincoln sisters had a different personality. Falcon was trigger happy, Dove was a book worm, Lily was creative, and Sage was damn near a hippy.

"Fuck no!" Mickey said as he straightened his stance and watched his woman. "I wifed her ass up that night, though." Falcon rounded the truck and leaned against the front of it and crossed her arms over her chest. She and Dove were practically twins, both short, dark, thick in every place that a man loved; she kept her hair short, cut like Toni Braxton does. Her eyes were a crazy-ass grey color that got darker when she got mad. The same tattoo Dove had on her leg; she wore on her right arm as a full sleeve. She wore the same matching joggers that Mickey wore, but in black, with a fitted red shirt and some red Tims on her feet. With her favorite gun tucked into the front of her pants.

"And yall been rocking ever since." I said more to myself than to him.

"We been rocking since we were young, we just stepped it up." Mickey said with a smirk on his face. "Aint no difference than you finally stepping up to Dove; you wanted shorty for a while before you finally made your move. Sitting in a fucking grad class learning about animals for a woman, you hardly said ten words to each time you saw her."

"How you know that?" I questioned with a laugh; I wasn't ashamed of shit I did. It wasn't like I was stalking the girl or anything; I just didn't want to rush shit with her.

"Nigga you don't think she told her sisters when she found out?" Mickey said with a laugh. "It was a whole group chat about your ass, they even told their mama and Constance, and when that happens then, that means the shit is real. Just know they got mad respect for you and they don't usually fuck with people and they fucking with you."

"Baby, I'm ready to go." Falcon said, looking over at Mickey, who only nodded his head. We slapped hands, pulled each other in for a quick hug, and released each other. Mickey made his way over to Falcon, stopping in front of her, pulled her close to him, and dropped a kiss on his lips before he walked her back around to her side of the car and opened the door for her.

"I'll let her have her fun with him and then call you and Trigga to finish the job." Mickey said as he opened his door and climbed behind the wheel of his car.

"Don't let her kill him." I said with a laugh.

"Nah, I promised yall that, and she agreed to it." Mickey said after closing his door, starting the car, and rolling down the window. "Be careful out there." I nodded my head at his comment and watched as they pulled off.

"That nigga Mickey got his hands full with that one." Benny said with a laugh as he unlocked the truck door. We all climbed in, including the chick from the house. She sat on the third row, looking out the window with her arms crossed over her chest.

"That nigga fell for a shooter he knew what he was signing up for." I responded with a laugh, I turned in my seat and looked at Trigga. "What you doing with shorty? You find out anything about her? Who her people? Shit what's her name"

"Nah, man, baby, ain't said two words since we been inside the house." Trigga said with a shake of his head; he lit his blunt that he left in the car earlier. "She going with me for a while." Trigga said, looking over at her. "Shit since she thinks she knows every fucking thing about me, Imma show her ass what a real gutta Miami nigga is like."

She turned to face him, not showing a sign of fear as she stared him down. "Nigga you don't put fear in my heart." She said to him with a look of disgust on her face. I let out a small laugh of my own when I turned around in my seat. She was that nigga problem now.

Dove

TWO MONTHS LATER...

I heard CJ come in the house; even though he wasn't loud, I still heard him. Without having to be with him, I knew his pattern; each time he stepped through the door after a long day, he did the same thing. He dropped his shoes by the front door and looked down to find his orange Nike slides, but I had them, so he probably laughed and sucked his teeth before putting on the black ones. He dropped his keys on the kitchen counter, then as he made his way through the room, he tapped on his iguana tank two times when he passed it. Like an old man, he let out a grunt as he took the few stairs that lead to the upstairs. As soon as he hit the top stair, he pulled his phone out and checked his security cameras to make sure the house is all clean. Once he was sure everything was all clear, he would walk down the hall and slowly open the door so that he wouldn't wake me. I smiled as he pushed the door open and waited for him to step foot inside the room.

"Shit, I didn't mean to wake you, baby." CJ said as he closed the door. I watched him closely; he didn't look tired or angry; if anything, he looked relaxed. He looked good in a pair of red True Religion shorts, a white tee that showed off his muscular body, a pair of white and red Jordan's, and as always, a custom-fitted KC fitted hat.

"You didn't; I was awake before you got here." I said as I adjusted the pillow I was using as support behind my back. "I didn't get to see you before you left this morning."

"I'm good baby." He said as he made his way towards me; he dropped his hat on the dresser as he passed it, then kissed me on my forehead. "Let me hop in the shower real quick." He kissed my lips this time then made his way towards the bathroom.

I watched without shame as he stripped his clothes off and put them in the laundry basket in the bathroom. Hell, if he was leaving the door open for me to peep in, he was mine and I looked every chance I got. He caught me watching him through the mirror; he let out a laugh before stepping into the shower and turning on the water. I kicked off the covers I was under and made my way to the bathroom.

"You not about to step in here and turn my water to hell." CJ said as soon as I opened the shower door. I watched as he dropped his head back and let the water run over his head, water clung to his short curly hair before dipping down on his beard.

"I won't adjust it." I said with a laugh as I stripped my clothes off and stepped inside. He stepped aside, letting me in; I grabbed my loofah and favorite body wash and began to lather my body. He watched me with low hooded eyes, licking his lips every so often but never said anything. Before CJ, I was sort of insecure about my body; I was a thick woman with a little bit of pudge, and most of the men I dealt with wanted a chick with a body like Cardi B, Nicki Minaj, or Meg Thee Stallion, and I didn't have that. "How was your day?"

"Tiring but I'm starting to get my second wind now." He said with a smirk on his face as he took my loofah from my hands and dropped it on the floor. He smiled at me as he stepped towards me; his dick was the first thing I felt poking me in the stomach before he gently gripped my throat and kissed me. I wrapped my arms around his neck and kissed him back; he bent down, grabbing me around my waist, and picked me up. I wrapped my legs around his body; it shocked me the first time he picked me up while we fucked in the shower a few weeks ago but now, each time he did it, I swear my pussy got wetter. He pulled his mouth from mine and kissed his way down my neck before biting me, then he kissed it to take some of the sting away. I dropped my head back, giving him better access.

"I missed you." He mumbled in my ear before biting down on it. "You miss me?"

"Yes." I panted; this was another thing that made me want him more. CJ was a talker, it didn't matter how much of a thug he was in the street; when we were together, he always told me how he felt. If he was angry at something I did, sad, hungry, happy, horny, it didn't matter. He expressed himself to me. When I mentioned it to him, he said that as a man, it was his job to let his woman know where he was at mentally when it came to their relationship. If he wanted to something different, it was his responsibility to communicate that with me just like it was mine when it came to him. He didn't believe in going to bed angry, and if he had a problem, he would wake my ass up and let me know, we would fix the problem, and then he'd dick me down so good I'd blackout.

"Open up for me then." He growled as he pushed himself inside me. I hissed in response as he waited, giving me time to allow my body to adjust to him. I held on tightly as he pushed in and out of me, each stroke hitting my favorite spot that only he knew about. "Give me two good nuts and I'll let you get your sleep before you have to be up for your graduation."

I let out a laugh because I knew he was lying; he never let me just give him two nuts. He rested his forehead against mine as he found his rhythm. I pulled his bottom lip into my mouth and bit down on it, he grunted and pumped harder into me. I released his mouth and dropped my head back, resting it against the shower wall as my first release hit me. My legs shook around his waist, and my pussy clamped down on his dick.

"That's one." He said as he unwrapped my legs from

him; once I was back on my feet, he spun me around and bent me over. I planted my hands on the shower floor and widened my legs, he bent down slightly, pulled my ass apart, and slid back into my pussy. He rocked into me so hard I almost slipped, but I caught myself by planting my hand on the wall. "Bounce that shit." He said and stopped moving.

I did as he instructed began to move my body to the beat that played in my head. I heard him groan a few times, letting me know that I was doing what he liked; I bit down on my lip when he started moving with me. The sound of our moans, the shower water running, and our skin slapping against each other was the only thing that could be heard. CJ bent forward and pulled me up by my shoulders making my back meet his chest. He pulled my face towards him and kissed me; his hips never stopped moving. My nut snuck up on me so fast that I had to pull away from him and moan as it took over me. Once it was over, he pulled out of me, and without looking back, he hit the handle that controlled the water and shut it off. I wiped the tears that fall from my eyes and watched him; he smiled at me before picking me up again.

"Okay I may have lied; you not getting away with just two nuts." He said as he stepped out of the shower with me in his arms. I laughed at him and shook my head; there was no doubt in my mind that he was going to have me hanging over the bed, begging him to let me go to sleep before the night was over. And my crazy ass wouldn't have it any other way.

10

Cj

"Dove Lincoln, Doctorates in Veterinarian Medicine." I hopped out of my seat, cupping my mouth, and let out a yell. I cheered as Dove walked across the stage with a big smile on her face. She had intentionally been the last one to walk because she knew we were going to make a lot of noise and interrupt anyone who went after her being so loud, but we didn't give a damn. Her sisters, aunt, and I were proud of what she'd accomplished, and we were going to be loud as hell for no reason than she deserved it. She shook the Dean's hand and accepted her diploma; she did a little shimmy after taking her picture and exited the stage. Dove didn't wait for the closing remarks or the announcement for them to turn their tassel; she made her way towards us.

"Congratulations baby!" Her Aunt Constance said with a smile on her face as she pulled her into a hug. They shared a few words just between them before each of her sisters congratulated her as well. I stood to the side, waiting for them to finish up, then pulled her into my arms and kissed her. I could hear in the background the Dean announce that they were officially graduates and to flip their tassels. I didn't even let her go when the crowd let out a loud cheer.

"It's sexy as hell to say I'm with a doctor." I said with a laugh finally letting her go, I took her hand in mine and we made our way through the maze of people who were now looking for their people since the graduation was officially over.

"Boy, you so stupid." Dove said with a laugh; I nodded my head at a few people as we passed them.

"We have somewhere to be real quick before we head to your party." I said as I opened the door for her. She raised her eyebrow in question but didn't say anything as she sat down in the seat. I closed the door, rounded the car, got in, started it, and rolled off. We drove for about thirty minutes to the outskirts of the city, I pulled up to an abandoned building and shut off the car.

"What's here?" She questioned as I reached behind her for the duffle bag that I put back there last night after she fell asleep.

"Your graduation gift." I replied, after I sat her bag in her lap, I pulled the other bag out that was for me. "Hurry up and change your clothes." I waited as she pulled the black joggers, yellow fitted tee, and black Tim's out of the bag. We had the same outfit, but our shirts were a different color. She looked over at me but didn't say a word; instead, she shrugged her shoulders, pushed her seat back to allow her more room, and did as I told her. Following her moves, I did the same, and we quickly changed our clothes and hopped out of the car. We made our way up the driveway, past the other cars parked along the way and I pulled the door open to get inside.

Hanging from a meat hook by his wrist in the middle of the building was Tika. Mickey, Falcon, Bleus, and

Trigga stood around him, talking and smoking a blunt.
Trigga's cousin Tiny had started to improve but wasn't out
of the hospital yet.

"What took yall so long to get here?" Mickey questioned as we slapped hands and pulled each other into
a hug.

"Not everyone speeds to get places man." I said in
responses as I made my rounds, getting everyone. I nodded
my head in the direction of Falcon and left it at that.
Mickey had already let me know to give her her distance
when she was in kill mode, so that's exactly what I did.

"You ready for this?" Falcon questioned her sister; they
stood side by side less than five feet from Tika's body. They
watched him sway back and forth but didn't speak for a
few seconds. Over the last two months, Falcon kept Tika in
this safe house. From what Mickey told me, she tortured
him physically and mentally.

"Nigga we dressed like the ghetto power rangers."
Benny said; I looked down at my clothes, then at everyone
else, and busted out laughing. He was right, we were
dressed alike, joggers, t-shirts, and Tim's. The only difference was our colors. Dove in yellow, I was in red, Trigga
was in blue, Benny was in green, Bleus was in black, and
Falcon was in all white. "Who decided on this shit?"

"Hell, man, I followed my woman's lead, this is the shit
she always wears when she's about to make some moves, so
I thought why not?" Mickey said with a laugh as he pulled
a blunt from his pocket. I wouldn't admit it to them but I
was the same way, it's been a while since I had to get my
hands dirty so I went with the easiest shit to change in and
out of. "You think she's going to do it?" Mickey questioned
me; instead of answering, we watched as Dove and Falcon
moved closer to Tika. He raised his head and smiled at her,
his front teeth were missing, and both his eyes were black.

It looked like he had a few open wounds running along his jaw, and flies were flying around his head, so I had no doubt they were eating away at him whenever they had the opportunity.

"Dove baby, you finally came to see me." Tika said, his head bobbed up and down as he tried to get his shit together. Even in his fucked up state he was still trying to impress her; shit was sad. "Come give me a kiss."

"Nigga you sad." Falcon said; she shook her head and pulled her gun from her waistband. "If you don't want to do this, it's fine, I'll let you walk away, and I'll do it for you." Falcon said, turning her attention to Dove, who hadn't taken her eyes off Tika yet. I was about to take a step towards Dove, but I stopped when I saw her take Falcon's gun from her.

"You picking that nigga over me?" Tika asked; it was like his mind snapped when he saw her reach for the gun. "You picking that nigga, after all, I've done for you? When nobody wanted your ass, who was there?! When you were crying over your stupid ass mama and punk ass daddy, who was there? Me! That's who and you gonna pick that nigga?" He yanked against his chains; spit flew from his mouth as he yelled at her. "That nigga not gonna love you like I did Dove!"

Calmly Dove walked towards him, she didn't even flinch when he jumped at her. Instead, she smiled at him, and for some reason, the nigga calmed down. She stood on her tippy toes and whispered something into his ear, which caused him to start yelling at her again. Dove took a step back, smiled at Tika again without a second thought raised the gun that Falcon had given to her, and blew his brains out. I watched with pride as my baby stepped around him, handed her sister her gun back, and made her way towards me. I took her hand, nodded at the fellas, and then to Falcon and we headed out the door.

"So what did you tell that nigga to have him going off on you like that?" I asked her as I put the car in drive and pulled off.

"I told him the truth, that even though he did all that shit, he was still a weak nigga, and Rose Lincoln didn't raise her daughters to be with weak niggas." She said, then she shrugged her shoulders and grabbed my hand. "Plus, I let him know your dick game was way better." I let out a loud ass laugh, then kissed her hand. I pressed down on the gas as we hit the highway, enjoying the peace we were experiencing as we rode. Dove reached over and turned the music up; her left hand looked a little bare but I ain't have no worries about that cause I planned to pop the question soon. I wasn't a fucking fool, yeah, I was a street nigga, but I knew a good woman when I saw one, and Dove was a damn good thing.

"Aye baby." I said; I turned down the music so she could hear me as I got off on the exit. She didn't say anything just looked up from her phone and waited. "You know you fell for the opp right?" Dove stared at me for a minute then fell over laughing.

"You a fucking fool, CJ." She said after she finally stopped laughing.

"Give me a kiss." I said to her, and she smiled that smile that is only for me and did just that.

Want to be a part of Grand Pens Publications??

To submit your manuscript to Grand Penz Publications, please send the first three chapters and synopsis to grandpenzpublications@gmail.com

Printed in Great Britain
by Amazon

43297783R00076